DOVER

XAVIER'S HATCHLINGS BOOK 5

KATHI S. BARTON

This is a work of fiction. Names, characters, places, and incidents are products of the author's imagination or are used fictitiously and are not to be construed as real. Any resemblance to actual events, locations, organizations, or persons, living or dead, is entirely coincidental.

World Castle Publishing, LLC
Pensacola, Florida
Copyright © Kathi S. Barton 2022
Hardback ISBN: 9798365540071
Paperback ISBN: 9781958336946
eBook ISBN: 9781958336953
First Edition World Castle Publishing, LLC, November 25, 2022
http://www.worldcastlepublishing.com
Licensing Notes
Cover: Karen Fuller
Editor: Karen Fuller

Prologue

Long ago, at a time when all creatures roamed the earth as only their true self. Working with and helping humans in whatever way they could. Where magic was celebrated. And dragons darkened the skies every day. It was then man figured out there was magic in the dragons and hunted them to almost extinction.

"I'm afraid there is no hope for us." No one made a sound as their leader continued. "Once the humans found out about us and what we can do for them dead, we have been doomed. I'm so terribly sorry."

Coop looked around the room. There were so few of them now he could easily count them. When he had been younger, thousands of years ago, there would not be enough room for all of them to share this room. Now they were down to having a quarter of them share the space because so many, his own wife included, had been murdered so needlessly. Coop was saddened by it all. Turning to leave the large cave, he was stopped by his brother, Xavier.

"The boys, they are well?" He nodded and smiled. Coop felt it all the way to his heart. A place had been dead for so long, it seemed. "You have the spell? You are going to use it on them? I should so wish I had thought of this before my own family was taken from me, Coop. You are a brave man and a good father."

"Thank you. And I shall use it tonight. It is the only way to save them." Xavier nodded, his own heart heavy with the losses they had suffered. "You know I would have shared should I have had it sooner. I am so sorry, brother. All of my heart, it's sorry for you."

"I know that. I do. But they are all gone now. My other half, my children. Killed for things are not fair to our kind." Coop knew all too well. "Aria was a good woman, Coop. A good woman and mother to your sons. She will be missed forever."

"Aye, in my heart and of my sons." Xavier stood there for several seconds, and Coop told him he must go. "They're waiting for word on what is to happen with us all."

"One more thing, if you please. It will not take but a second. I have left them all I have. It is where you keep them hidden away, the boys. Deep within the cave, it's all there." Coop asked him what he meant. "I cannot go on, brother. I cannot. There is too much grief in my heart for me to live. I have left my things for them there. They might survive this; with the magic you have to give to them. And if so, they'll need more than you have to help them."

"Xavier, please, you mustn't do this. They'll miss you as much as I." Xavier nodded and said it had begun. "You can come and stay with us. You'll live with us in the caves."

"Nay. I cannot. I must go. Just tell them I love them. With all of my heart." There would be no stopping him once his heart was made up, Coop knew this, but it made his heart no less full for it. "Good bye, my brother. Take care you are not caught by the humans."

Coop made his way back to his hidden cave and sat before the fire. The boys, he knew, were resting, their bodies getting stronger daily with their age. Soon they would be as big as him, a dragon of worth and size. When his eldest son came to him, his eyes full of fear, Coop knew it was well past time he did what he had been practicing. The magic would keep them safe.

Gathering his sons, six of them of varying shades of blues and greens, he asked them to have a seat. He had a story to tell them. It was not a story, not truly, but a tale that would hopefully keep them safe.

"A witch told me once of a great magic only few can do. It takes a loving heart and a strong dragon to make it work. I have asked her, and she has told me how to make it so. In this magic, it will keep you all safe from the humans." They nodded, each of them knowing it was a human blade that took the life of their dear mother. "I will perform this upon you, each of you, at the same time and give you some magic you will use when you need it. This magic, strong and powerful magic, will let you roam with the humans, and they'll not know your true self is just below your flesh."

"You mean we'll be humans as well?" He nodded, then shook his head at Cooper, his oldest. "I don't understand, father. Will you explain?"

"Yes. The magic I will give you will let you change into your true self when you are alone. But when you are out in the world, you will need to be a human. A man." Cooper looked at his brothers and then back at him as he continued. "With this magic, I will also give you a gift. Something you will need to keep yourself safe should they find out. A stronger armor than any other dragon before you as well as the same immortality you have now, as man or dragon."

Hudson stared at him for long moments. He was the thinker, and if he could think of a reason for this not to work, he would voice it loudly. He was much like his mother in that. She would be the first to say when she did or did not like something. And the first to say the plan was perfect. He only hoped she would have approved of this.

"I think you are very smart, father. To try and keep us safe. But I can only think this will not work on you. Or is your plan?" The boy was much too smart, Coop thought. "If you change us, who will change you?"

"There will be no one to change me, son. I will... It is my wish to join your mother in this earth." He watched them, seeing if they understood the love he had lost when she had been murdered. "Giving you this magic, it will be something I can tell her I've done for her sons. You know as well as I that she loved you more than anything on this earth, including herself."

"She died saving us." Coop nodded at Lincoln. "I'm not happy you're going to die, father, but I understand wanting to be with mother. I miss her more every day."

"As do I." He looked at his sons, all of them growing into dragons of worth. "I must have an agreement from you all. Even if one of you does not want this, then it will not work. I would say you should think on this hard. For once, I have given this to you, there will be no going back."

"I wish to have it." He knew Cooper would be the first. Not that he did not love his father, but Cooper would see things in a way most would not. To not have this done would mean a certain death for them all. Dragons were too valuable dead not to be hunted for all time. "I will do whatever it takes to make sure you are proud of me as well."

"I am already, Cooper. Forever." The others nodded too. They were ready for this as much as he was dreading it. Because once he started the process of changing his sons into men, then he would begin to die. It would take all he was to change them.

Standing up, spreading his wings out behind him, Coop told them about the things their uncle had left them. They knew where the family jewels were, the things their mother had left them as well. Once they were standing, their bodies strong and healthy, he felt his heart swell and break for what he was about to do.

"I, Cooper Manning, of the Manning Dragons of the earth, give to my sons, Cooper, Hudson, Lincoln, Lucas, Tristan and Xavier, all I am. Each of you will take a part of the earth with you when you are converted. The part of you that is unique in all ways will be strengthened and enhanced. You will be immortal, forever, and those you take to your heart will be as well." His sons bowed before him when he told them to. He said the words over them that would change them into men. Coop could feel his body shutting down, his heart beating a little less. But he had one more thing he wished to bless them with and held himself upright to give it from his own dying heart. "One day, true love will come to you. And you will have more than you have ever known. It will fill you in ways you cannot ever imagine. Love will be yours for all times. For only then will you become a true dragon, a Manning Dragon."

~*~

Cooper sat with his brothers while their father lay dying. His heart was weak from what he had done, and it was tearing him apart. Father was weak, yes, but he continued to tell them tales of their mother, of their adventures when they were only small dragons. They were going to be alone soon; their father was so close to joining their mother that it hurt Cooper in ways he had not expected.

"What shall we do with his body?" Cooper looked at Tristan and asked him what he meant. "He will not be able to lie here. If the humans were to find him, they will surely cut him up into pieces. I do not want that for him. We were never able to bury mother in the proper way after what they did to her."

"We could burn his body." Cooper wondered how it would work when Hudson continued. "His scales will be worthless to them should they come upon his body. The magic he held within him also will be useless to them. He will be nothing more than a carcass. They'll leave alone."

Burn his body. It was something to think about. But he did not want to, not while he was still breathing, his body still alive. When he laid his head upon his father's chest, hearing his heart beating slower and slower, Cooper wondered what his father would think if he knew the magic he had given them had not worked. They were all still as dragons.

"He gave his life to keep us safe. But it did not work." No one said anything to him as they each watched their father. "Dragons such as we are, we'll be hunted and killed by the humans. There is nothing we can do but wait for them."

"We will survive if we stay here." Cooper told Xavier they would have to leave here eventually. "To feed and to fly, yes. But perhaps we could do it only at night. To keep to the skies and not let them see us."

"They know we are about and will have spies

out looking for our lairs. We will have to kill any man should he come for us, and still, we will not be safe. We are, after all, dragons who have a great deal of magic." Cooper stopped breathing.

Cooper did not hear his father's heart and knew it was at an end. He was quiet for a bit longer, waiting, hoping for just one more beat. One more sound would mean he was still alive. But there was nothing. Their father was dead. Sitting up, he told them he had passed this world into the next.

None of them had ever seen a dragon die before. Their mother had been dead when they found her. Each dragon they had come upon when they were out had been dead long before they found them. Their bodies were stripped of every part, so they resembled less of a dragon than just a pile of bones.

Their scales were used for roofs for their homes and for shields. The very meat of them was roasted and stored away so it could be used for medicines and potions. Hearts were cut up and dried, then ground into a powder to use for other things the humans would use to keep them from sickness, as well as magic to have a grand garden and trees heavy with fruit. The only part that would be left was the bones, and sometimes even those were carried off and used for something. Cooper hated all humans.

"We will do as suggested by Hudson. It is the only assured way we can—" Before he could finish, he felt the stirring of the earth. It shook so hard it knocked each of them off their feet. As they lay there, terrified someone was coming for them, their father appeared before them.

His body was still aground. But instead of dark in death, he was brilliant in light. Faeries, thousands upon thousands of faeries, seemed to be covering him. Before Cooper could tell them to stop, to leave him alone, father spoke.

"I love you, my sons." Each of them nodded. Fear was almost something he could touch. "I will now and forever join my true love, your mother. I must warn you when you find your other half, and you will, you will have to be careful of the slayers. They will know what you have found by the magic you both will share. My sons, you will leave this place and take your place among men. Becoming someone I will be proud of."

"Father, the magic didn't work. We're still a

dragon." Cooper felt shameful to say a thing to his father. To tell him his sacrifice had not worked. "We will be hunted and killed."

"Nay, you only need to think of being your other half. Becoming a man is simple. The same when you wish to be your true self." Cooper was not sure what he meant, but his father continued before he could ask. "Go, now before men come here. The magic to hide me will draw them here. Be safe, my sons and know I love you more than I do any other creature on this place."

Cooper stood then. The faerie was still working, taking the body of his father apart. But as he watched, he could see they were not doing anything but preserving his body. Faerie ropes were all around him, and strings of magic were wrapped around him like a cocoon. It made him invisible to all. As Cooper stood there, his brothers beside him, he knew, like him, they mourned the loss of yet another parent.

"You are the eldest?" He nodded to the faerie when she asked. "We have a gift for you. For all of you, but you will receive the most. Your father was a great man, your mother a queen among her people. We wish to bestow upon you all your father had."

"My brothers, they will need it as well. I should like to share." She smiled at him and bowed. "What have you done with his body?"

"He is being prepared to be moved. We will make a grand garden upon him. Flowers will be there for all to see, but only few will know a dragon is there with his other half, his love." He nodded. It was as it should be. "You will take this gift? You will share, but as I said, you will get more than the others."

"I don't care. Please, just do what you must so we can hide." She nodded again and touched her fingers, small, tiny ones, to his forehead. Then she did the same to the others before coming back to him. "It is done? You have shared it with us?"

"I have, Lord Cooper. But you must leave here now. There are humans coming. The magic we used to do this thing has given them cause to come here." He nodded and looked at the ground where their father had been. "He is safe. Just as your mother is now. Go before they find you here and murder you as well."

He thanked her for her help and left. The exit from this part of the cave was hidden so well that only they knew about it. As they made their way into the night, he thought of the human inside of him, and the pain of it took his breath away. In seconds, he was down on his knees. Whatever was happening, he was surely going to die.

"You're a man." He looked up at his brothers as they began to transfer to one themselves. "We'll be safe now, all of us. We'll be humans for them until we can find a place where we can be ourselves."

"I don't think that's ever going to happen again." Hudson nodded and held his head tightly as he did so. "We will need to train ourselves in their ways. Become what they are. But never monsters."

"No, never." They made their way to a building; any would do for now. Hudson, like him, was staggering a little, but they were getting stronger as they moved. He turned to look at him as they were settling into the empty shell of a house. "We will need to buy things, houses and such."

"Yes. But tomorrow. I am too tired to think beyond how much we have lost." Hudson and the others agreed. "When the humans are gone from our cave, we'll go and find what father was telling us about earlier, about the wealth will keep us safe."

"I only hope there is a great deal of it. I don't know how to work nor drive." Cooper told Xavier, the youngest brother, they would soon learn. "I hope so. I hope so."

He did as well. It was going to be hard enough for them to learn to eat and dress like them, much less get around. Cooper hoped this worked. For he was as afraid as he had ever been in his life.

~*~

After a time, thousands of years, each of the dragons turned into men and forged their way into a world that was so different than the one they had been born into. It seemed a different planet. But survive, they did.

Having their mates come to them, children born to all of them, gave them hope. A small and fragile thing after such hardships they were born to. Cooper became, as his father had been before him, the king of dragons. His mate, Carson, their queen. It had been and still is a time for celebration. To this day, they commemorate often and hard at each new birth of the dragons turned men and women.

The others, his brothers, prospered too. Finding

their other half, making their magic stronger for having their love. They worked hard to keep everyone safe and well fed. Humans or other dragons. No one, not anyone in need, would have ever been turned away from their help. The Manning Dragons, true to their father and mother, became the most powerful dragons ever born.

Of the six sons, Xavier's sons, four hatchlings, and two humans moved far away to be the next generation of Manning dragons who would open their hearts and doors for all creatures. Even the sons of their hearts, the two human-born men carried a powerful magic. They used it with their brothers to help as many people as possible, humans and dragons alike, to live in the ever-changing world. To help them not only succeed but to perhaps help someone else when they needed it. These boys, now men, have stories to tell.

Chapter 1

George tried not to look at the webpage he was on. Instead, he focused on what was before him, whatever the hell it was. Laughing a little at his inability to keep himself occupied, he looked again at the time left. Forty-seven minutes and twelve seconds.

"What are you doing?" He looked up to see Milo had entered the room at some point. "You're very distracted. I asked you if you had the pictures that were on the table last night when I left."

"I'm bidding on something." He looked at the time left, the only thing he could see of the auction. "There are still forty-six minutes left. Christ, I think my timer is broken."

"What are you bidding on?" Milo sat down but looked distracted too. "I came here to work out an issue I'm having with my story so far. Maybe you can distract me enough that I can figure it out on my own."

"It's a bunch of teapots. Six of them, as a matter of fact. They're very ugly if you only bought them for their beauty. But one of them is calling to me." Milo asked him what it was saying. He knew his brother, this one anyway, would understand what he was saying. "It's telling me I need to purchase it at any cost. Believe it or not, it then told me to be reasonable about it."

Milo came around to his side of the desk, asking for a view of them. Not wanting to know if he was winning or not, George pulled up the catalog to show them to him. Milo looked at the three pictures that were showing what was in the set.

"They're pretty ugly, George. Do you suppose it is something that just wants to be in a forever home?" George told him it would be if he paid his top dollar for it. "What is your top dollar for it? Since they're listed as a single item, I'm assuming whatever you pay will be times one?"

"No, six. They make that very clear in the description. My highest bid is fifty thousand. That seemed reasonable to me." Milo whistled. "I know. It's not reasonable at all, is it? I just need to see what it wants from me."

Again, Milo seemed to understand what he was saying. Glancing at the clock again, he would see that he'd used up ten minutes of his time. He told Milo how much time was left.

"Can I stay with you while it's going on? I won't tell anyone about the price you have on it, but what's the starting point for them?" He told him. "Okay, so best case scenario is that you pay sixty cents for them. Worst case, you pay fifty grand. How much time is left now?"

"Twenty-nine minutes." This was better. He should have asked Milo to come and keep him sane sooner. "I was looking through some of the catalogs I have for other auctions that are supposed to be for an old estate. The contents on this estate auction are supposed to have been around for seven generations. I wouldn't have any idea about it, but the teapot asked me to come and bid on it. The other things, like a couple of large pieces from the Ming Dynasty, are in the collection as well. Teapots, even uglier ones than this one, go for big bucks online."

They talked about the food pantry, the one he was working on. "I went to a few of the businesses and started this contest for canned goods. The business that gets the most gets a dinner out for all their employees. Mom said not to make it pizza, but something along those lines. Dad said to make it a gift card with an amount on it. That way, they could decide on what it was they want to have for their meal." He laughed a little. "The bank in town has only eight employees, and the insurance company had fifteen. But I bet the bank will win simply because they'll be the underdog in this."

"I like that idea. Did you say what sort of canned goods we wanted? I mean, even boxed food like mac and cheese would be enough to fill a few bellies." Milo said he'd revise it to include boxed things as well. "Also, tell them that they can have the public help them along by picking their favorite place to have people bring by something for the box. That would get the people on the streets involved as well."

Milo made notes, and George looked at the timer. He sighed heavily and looked at his brother, telling him the bidding for the teapots had ended. Being too scared and excited to look on his own, he asked Milo to have a look for him.

It took a little longer than he wanted for Milo to figure out where the bidding prices were. Before he could get it pulled up, George's phone rang. It was the auction house. Making his brother answer it, he wanted to brain him before he finally hung up.

"What did you agree to? Bank draft for the amount. Mom is going to kill me, isn't she? How much? No, don't tell me. I don't want to know either that I didn't win—" Milo put his hand up, and George shut up. "Just fucking tell me."

"Mr. Daniels asked if we wanted to come by and pick it up. After finding out that it was only a few miles from here, I told him we would. Secondly, he wanted to know if you'd continue being a patron of his auction house. I guess you get a discount on the things you buy from them if you're on their mailing list. I told them you'd do that when we were there." George asked him how much again. "Less than we thought at thirty—"

"Mom is going to kill me. I just hope I can appease her by the pot being worth some bucks. Or it tells me where I can take it to be sold to someone stupider than I am." Milo laughed. "I don't find this the least bit funny, Milo. I'm going to tell your wife you hit me. She loves me."

"She loves me more. And I get to sleep with her." Milo smiled. "I didn't say thirty grand, you moron. I was going to say thirty cents. You got them all for thirty cents because you're going to become a patron of the place. The first time you use your new status, you can take fifty percent off items of less than a hundred dollars. So you got— Are you all right, George?"

"Are you fucking kidding me right now? Thirty fucking cents? That's all I paid for them?" Milo said he'd not paid for them yet, but when they went to get them, then he could— George cut his brother off. Again. "You fucking dick. If this is just a joke on your part, I'm not going to be responsible for what I do to you. It's all on you."

"Pull up your email. They said they were sending you the invoice right away." He was shaking so badly he had to put his password in three times before he got it to work. "Just breathe, George, before Winnie shows up and hurts me because you're hyperventilating."

Taking a calm breath in and out, he nodded. Then he put in his password and waited for the connection. As soon as he was able to open his email, the invoice was there. He'd gotten them for less than a buck even with premium price added in, as well as taxes.

"I don't believe this." Milo asked him if he was ready to go. "To pick them up? Of course. Just let me — you know what, we'll go now. I was going to tell Mable that I was going out for a while, but I'll just call her when we get on the road. Because you kept me from being insane, I'll buy you dinner."

"Deal. Pem and Jamie were called into the hospital to perform surgery on a kid that *fell out of a tree.* Neither one of them are buying that just so you know. But his leg is broken in two places, and his arm has been shattered. Jamie told me it looked like he'd been hit with a hammer a couple of times." He asked who it was. "I don't know. She doesn't ask, so I don't know until she finds out for me. But we're going to be paying a visit to someone as soon as we find out. No one needs to beat up on a ten year old. Not like this."

They were on the highway in ten minutes. He's forgotten to print off his invoice, but since he had it on his phone, George thought it would be all right. Even if it wasn't, he was going to take them home, even if he had to steal them away. Laughing, he told Milo what he'd been thinking.

"You do that, and I'm not going to protect you. You do realize that Mom and Dad are both living here now. They won't care how old you are. Mom will make you feel terrible, and Dad will give you that look." George asked him what look. "You know it. The one where he's thinking that he needs to blame himself for your downfall. That he'd raised you better than that, and he's simply a failure. You've seen it. I know I have."

"I remember it now. Sort of a cross between a basset hound and a sad sack." They both laughed, then both of them looked around in the event one of their parents had heard them. "Milo, I have to tell you. All Mom or Dad have to do is say my name in that way they do, and I'm scrambling to find a solution to whatever it is I've done, without any thought to be being nearly three hundred years old. As well as a grown assed man."

"Me too. I don't know where needing to feel sorry came from either. It's like we're ingrained with it from birth or something." They were both still laughing as they pulled into the parking lot. "Are you all right? I'm going to go in with you to look around. I might get rid of some of the shit I've accumulated over the years. A lot of it is just furniture I bought old in the first place. So it'll be ancient by now."

"That's a great idea. I've been paying on several storage lockers since — well, I don't know how long. But keeping it on the off chance it may come back in style is stupid. Maybe I can use the money to get some things I really want. Not that I can think of what that would be right off the top of my head, but I could put it aside."

They were shown to a large room and asked to have a seat less than thirty minutes after George won the bid. They didn't know what was going on, but George didn't like this, so he checked into the mind of the man who had spoken to him last week. When he came into the room, George decided to wait to be told rather than accuse them of some kind of under dealing when it came to his pots.

"We've had two of your teapots stolen, Mr. Manning." George had known this, of course, but hearing it coming out of his mouth was altogether different. "We, of course, are devastated at the loss and will make it up to you in any way you see fit."

"Can he see which teapots are left?" The man was falling all over himself to tell Milo that would be just wonderful. If he said "wonderful" once more, George was going to hit him in the mouth. As soon as the man was out the door, Milo turned to him. "They might not have taken the one you want. However, I'd make sure he knows how disappointed you are. This isn't any way to run a business. It's only been about a half-hour. I have to think it was an inside job."

"You're more than likely right on that. Someone just waiting on the off chance they could get them without paying for them. But why?" Milo shrugged. "I'm too upset to look. You do it before I rape the mind of every person in here." Milo nodded to him as soon as Mr. Deaver came back into the room. His pot was still there, and it was all he could do not to take it and run. "Are you doing an investigation into this?"

"He doesn't need to, George. He's the one that took it. Mr. Deaver here is responsible for a lot of other theft in this place. Mostly it's on groupings like the one you purchased, and he'll help himself to one or two of the pieces and say they were stolen. When in actuality, they're in his office right now, sitting on his desk. Aren't they, Phillip?" Phillip started to back out of the room, and when he was at the doorway, Winnie was there to capture him. "These men are here to arrest him. The rest of his stash of stolen items is in his home. George paid for two more teapots that are in the office here."

"Thanks, guys. I've been having reports run across my desk since I've been here. I had no idea it was anything more than just petty theft. This takes it to a whole new level with there being so many other things taken." Winnie smiled at them both. "I love this gig, by the way. Helping out the police department for a little while."

Deaver was read his rights and taken away. Right out the front door where everyone could see him being arrested.

Winnie was watching the police department

while the man in charge of the place was on a two-week vacation. George thought she was having a good deal more fun than she should have been, but it was working out. George had a feeling that if the man didn't return, his aunt would do the job for free. She was having so much fun.

"I think she's enjoying this so much. She might live here too." George thought the same thing. "What do you think she thinks is fun about it?"

"I don't know. Also, I'm not sure others would think what she's doing is called *fun*. I think crime is down by a great deal, not that there was much here anyway. And there have been fewer fights at the bars nightly." Milo said that was what she was more than likely enjoying. The feel of accomplishment. "I think you might be right. Not many dragons are fucking up nowadays, and people, for the most part, still don't believe in them. Maybe she's just bored."

"Could be." An officer brought him in the final two teapots. Them being in person didn't improve their looks at all. George thought they might be uglier now that he could see them. "Christ, what was I thinking?"

Open me. George looked at Milo and asked him

if he'd heard it too. When he nodded, both of them sat down with the teapot between them. *Take off this stuff so I can breathe again, Young George. I need my air.*

The outside of the pot was polymer clay that had been baked at a very low temperature to make it seem harder than it really was. Carefully pulling the chunks away from the teapot, George could see that it was jade. Very old and very dark jade.

"George?" He sat back and looked at the piece when ninety percent of the clay was pulled free. "That's a dragon. I don't know if you can tell or not, but that looks like our grandma. Our Dad's mother. Weren't we told she was a jade-colored dragon?"

~*~

No one touched the teapot. It was beautifully done, Jamie thought. The way someone had etched the dragon into the entire pot, using her tail for the handle and her mouth for the spout, made her think whoever had done this had seen an actual dragon. Even the clawed feet that made up the pot's footer was as realistic as anything she'd ever seen. Jamie had even nicked her finger on one of the claws that curved up and down on it.

The detail was exquisite. The colors of the carved areas were done in such a way it enhanced the three-dimensional dragon rather than take away from it. The writing on it, something that she had no idea how to read, was carved in the greatest detail she'd ever witnessed.

"I love the attention to detail on all of it. But the fact that they carved the dragon, so it looks more like it's resting on the teapot rather than a part of it, is what makes me think someone knew what they were doing in hiding it. The gold tips of the scales makes her look like she's resting after a long flight." Jamie had to agree. The sole reason for hiding it in plain sight had to be very telling. She asked Xavier if it was true, that it was his mother. "I don't know for certain. I will tell you I've not thought of my mom as much as I used to. It's been longer than I care to think on at times. I was the youngest of the six, so I don't have as many memories as the others do. But I do remember my uncle telling me once that there was a human that did carvings and that my mom had been asked to sit for him. I don't know what it was she sat for, but I'm reasonably sure this could be her."

The top of the lid had a broken egg, decorated with not just diamonds but emeralds as well. The gold used carefully had been used as highlights. The circle around the egg was where they found the smallest dragon just outside the broken shell of its birth. The tiniest slivers of emeralds in the larger dragon's eyes seemed to be able to follow a person around the room. Winnie had even unearthed six equally beautiful teacups from the stash of Deaver that had golden rings around the cup's rim to sit it level on any surface. No handles were on the cups, and it took her a few moments to realize they'd not been broken off but had never been on it.

Asking and being told that she could pick it up, she was surprised at how light it was. Not paperweight light, but not nearly as heavy as she had assumed it would be. Putting it back on the table, she asked George if he'd had any more conversations with it.

"Not yet. It told me it was finally free to breathe and that she'd talk to me later, but nothing more than that. How much do you think it's really worth? Not that it matters—I'm just glad to have it." George laughed a little. "You don't seem surprised that I can talk to things."

"Did Uncle Cooper say when he was coming by to see it? I mean, he's the oldest. Maybe he has some insight on it." Milo asked what he'd missed. "Oh, I told Jamie about your ability when we were talking one night."

"He said he was on his way. That's all he said." George sat across from Milo as he continued. "You have no idea how much I want to make a cup of tea in this thing. Just to see it pour into one of the cups. And then taste it. I don't know what I'm expecting it to taste like, but I'm hoping it'll be as close to what this thing looks like in magnificence."

"Why don't you? I mean, it's a teapot, right? You should do it." George told Jamie he wanted Cooper to see it first. That way, if it was his mom, he thought all of the brothers should have the first pot. Jamie was visibly impressed as she told George that. "Wow, that's really sweet of you, George. Who would have thought you were a romantic like that?"

"Don't get used to it. I'm trying to get brownie points to use later. Having an uncle king of your kind surely does put a damper on your life at times." They were laughing when the front door was opened. As soon as they realized it was Cooper and Carson, each of them stood up. Even Jamie did. "Uncle Cooper, I found something today. Well, three weeks ago, but I didn't get it until today. I wasn't going to —" Someone cleared their throat. "I'm sorry. I'm just really nervous. Did your mom really pose for a man that did jade carvings? That's important to know."

"Yes. I don't remember the man's name, but yes, she did it. In exchange for her sitting for him, she was able to take as many sheep as she wished, so long as she didn't take them all, to feed us boys with. I think there were times when that was all there was between us starving or not. Why do you ask?" George moved out of the way, and Cooper looked around the room before looking at the teapot. "Holy shit, George. Holy shit. It's Mom. I'd know that carving anywhere. He brought it to the cave we were living in and showed it to us. It was so tiny to us then, nothing more than a speck in his palm. But that's it."

Cooper asked if he could touch it. "Yes, of course. I don't know what the writing says at the bottom of it, but the cups were found by Aunt Winnie. She found them when someone tried to steal them—" He caught himself again. "It spoke to me. From the catalog. It begged me to pay any price to purchase it. Then it went silent other than to ask me to remove the polymer clay that was baked around it to hide it, I guess."

"It says here…." Cooper had to sit down, and he held the teapot to his heart. "It says *To my favorite dragon. I have named her Ava.* That was my mother's name from then on. Ava." He wiped at the tears, and Jamie could feel her own eyes filling with unshed emotions. "Have you told the others yet? What did Xavier say about it?"

"He didn't know." Cooper turned to his younger brother and asked him about it. He said the same thing to his elder brother as he had to them. He just didn't remember her. George continued. "I was just telling Jamie here that you and the others should be the ones that use it first. I want you to tell me in great detail how it tastes, too."

They were laughing as Winnie and Hudson, now that he was there, gathered up the other uncles. Like Cooper, they were moved to tears at the sight of the little teapot, and Jamie had to go and get boxes of tissues for the family.

Jamie had learned to make tea the Chinese way when she'd been in college. One of her roommates had been from a very traditional family, and she'd learned from her great grandmother. She did that now to show them she had as much knowledge of the jade teapot as they did. Not their mother, of course, but of the pouring tea ritual.

When the tea was ready, she told Cooper, as head of the household back when it was just the six of them, and waited while he sipped the tea, holding the tiny looking cup in his big strong hands. He sat his cup down, having only taken a sip. Cooper burst into tears as soon as his brothers did the same with his cup.

"I'll pay you ten times what you paid for it, George. I won't take no for an answer, either. I would love to be able to pull this out when I need a pick me up, and share it with my family. On special occasions, of course. Ten times what you paid is a lot of money." Milo laughed so hard it was difficult not to join him. "Have I missed something?"

"Ten times is a very reasonable amount, George. If nothing else, you should be happy he's not making you hand it over." Cooper said he'd not do that for any amount of money. Their uncle Lincoln said he was trying to make a point. That made Milo and George laugh all the harder. "I don't see what is so funny."

"You can have it for ten times what I paid for it, Uncle Cooper." George, still fighting laughter, handed his uncle the bill of sale. "With the six teapots I got, that comes to five cents each. So you owe me fifty cents. I don't know how much the cups were—they were brought here by Winnie when she found the other things in the man's office—but they're yours anyway. For the price of telling me how the tea tasted."

They were all laughing then, and Cooper asked her if she'd make more tea for the others. She was glad now that she'd paid attention to her friend and remembered that rushing a good cup of tea was the same as rushing through a shitty job at painting. The art of it was lost.

They all had a cup of the delicious brew. Cooper didn't sip the second time but stared into the cup. Jamie asked him if he could read tea leaves.

He smiled at her. "I can, but I don't know how good at it I am. The last time I did it was when I was just a young dragon. The man who carved this gave each of us a cup and then read our leaves. Mine said that I was destined for great things. All my mind could think of was being like my father, king of all dragons. I guess it came true." He dumped his leaves onto the surface of the table after drinking the tea and stared down at them. "It says I'm going to live a long and very fruitful life. That usually means children. That I'll have enough good fortune that I will forever have a spark to light the fire and enough sense to get in out of the rain." He looked at it harder. "I'm sorry, I read it wrong. It says I'll have enough sense to know that water is the root of both evil and good. That's about right, I think."

They took turns having their leaves read by Cooper. He enjoyed it as much as the rest of them did. When it was time for supper, Cooper and Carson took them all out. Telling them not to get used to him being such a generous man, he hugged George to him.

"This is far and away the best thing that someone has given me and the rest of my brothers, George. I don't know what to say about how you've made me feel." George told him it would be his pleasure for him to just take it. That giving it to him had been his plan all along. "Thank you. I'll make it up to you."

"Before I forget." Jamie stood next to Milo as he looked at his uncle. "I've been given a new job, as I'm sure you know from my mom. But she asked me to make sure I let you know what I've...what Jamie and I have done for this family. The ability to have children that aren't dragons, but will have some of their traits, is now there for any of us second generation to have."

No one moved. They did look at Milo like he had a second head or something. Finally, it was Xavier that stood up and thanked them. Then it was a free for all on all of them hugging the two of them. It was Finn that thanked him the most.

"A child of her own? You've no idea how much she's been wanting one. Rachel has never said anything, but I can feel her sadness every night when she's supposed to be sleeping. I don't know what you did to make this happen, Milo and Jamie, but I owe you everything right now. There isn't a thing I'd not do for you or even pay you for the happiness I feel right now." Milo told them what they'd done and how Gem had told them what a wonderful job they'd done for her and her kind. "This is wonderful. You've no...

well, I guess you do have an idea. That's wonderful."

"Also, we're going to have a child too. A daughter."

More cheers went up, and there was much hugging from everyone. Even though Xavier and Cindi knew, they acted like they were given the news for the first time ever. Jamie certainly did love this family and their ways of making a person feel so welcomed and a part of something larger than she'd ever had before.

After everyone left, she and Milo sat on the couch and enjoyed the evening air from the open doors in the living room. She didn't need to have television to watch. No job was pressing her. All she had was her thoughts. Until the little boy and his accident of falling out of the tree returned to her mind.

She turned to tell Milo what she knew and found him sound asleep. Even his face was so relaxed that he had his mouth open, and soft snores mingled with the sound of his heart as it beat in his chest. Jamie realized in that moment that she was indeed in love with Milo Manning and wondered why it had taken her so long to realize he was the most important person in her life. And would be forever.

When she snuggled up to him, he wrapped his arm around her and pulled her closer to his body. In seconds, less she thought, she was beginning to feel her own body relaxing. Soon she knew she'd be as asleep as he was.

~*~

Toby hung up the phone when she didn't find a phone number for George Manning. She didn't know why she thought the man could help her, but since her uncle had finally been arrested, she was going to go out on a limb and find out if he knew what he'd gotten in the way of the pretty teapots. Also, she was told he'd gotten the handleless cups that had gone with it.

Being the one that had covered the teapot in the clay, she wanted to make sure he knew what a treasure it was that he'd purchased. The fact that he got it for such an ungodly low amount thrilled her to no end. People like her uncle, Donald Deaver, were better off not being born.

Just as she was getting ready to call it a day, she saw a couple walking down the street across from her. Toby wasn't sure how she thought it was a Manning or even why she did, but she crossed the street at the light.

As soon as she stepped in front of the two of them, she felt the hairs on the back of her neck dance.

"You're not human." Neither of them said anything, but they did stiffen a little. "I know you have no idea who I am or that you should care, but I'm the niece of Donald Deaver. My name is Toby Deaver. I want to say up front that I'm glad he was finally arrested. However, I do have some information on one of the teapots you purchased."

"Why is it you think that we purchased anything from your uncle, Toby?" The woman wasn't nasty, but Toby would bet in a second that she could be if crossed. "My name is Imp Manning. This is my mate, George. He's a dragon since you know we're not human, so I'd watch my next words if I were you."

Nodding, she said that she would. "How did I know? Well, you're not going to believe me, or perhaps you will if he's really a dragon, but it told me that you purchased it. Like, I knew you were the ones that bought it too. Well, the mister was. You weren't around when she was given to a man by the name of Cooper Manning." She thought about what she sounded like and was glad they didn't run her off. Yet, anyway.

"The little one, uglier than the others, had some clay around it. I put that on there when she asked me to do it. I know this sounds like I'm off my noodle, but I swear to you, that's what she told me to do."

"I believe you." Toby was sure she could have hugged the man for saying that to her. But she didn't. There was trouble afoot, as her grannie said, and she needed to explain something to him. "Did it happen to tell you why you were to cover it up?"

"So that Donald the Asshole didn't know what he was putting out there. He would have stolen it, too, had someone not, I'm assuming you, figured it out. But the pot told me that you were the one that was to get her. She said she talked to you before the auction." George asked her if she was hungry as they were headed to dinner. "I'm sorry. But I'm not wealthy or anything. I can't afford the places you're sure to go."

"Actually, I should have said that I'd pay." She looked back at her car, then at the man. "Is she with you? She can come with us as well. I'm sure you've talked to her about this."

"My grannie. And my son, Shawn Deaver. Grannie is my uncle's mom." Grannie got out of the car with Shawn and looked at herself in the car mirror before crossing the street. Shawn wouldn't have let go of Grannie's hand even if she begged him to. He loved her as much as Toby did. When someone nearly ran her down, she smacked the hood of their car and told them to slow the fuck down. "She's not at all what someone would think of when they think of a grandma. She's outspoken, rude at times, and has a mind of her own. But she's mine, and I love her to pieces. So does my son."

"This should be a very enjoyable meal, then." As they were seated, Imp explained to her that they'd just gotten back from a much needed vacation. "It was only two days, but I feel as if I've been handed the world."

The chatter, what she thought of as small talk, wasn't boring. When Imp could, she included her grannie in the conversation and even asked them about where they were staying. Grannie had been warned not to tell people about their situation. She might well have told her to tell her for all the good it did to ask Grannie to hush. Shawn sat in her lap when they were seated.

"Right now, we're staying in the car. Not as bad

as it sounds. They're roomy seats, and we're not all that big. My son is an asshole. Both of them were, but Toby's dad, he's in prison. Jackass tried to rob one of them armored cars when it was just sitting at a light one day." Toby put her hand over her face and watched the reaction of the people she'd come to warn. Shawn pointed out that Grannie was going to have to be in time-out. "When that pot called out to my Toby here, she said we'd have to go right then. Been three days of sitting around waiting for one of you guys to show up. Now that you have, perhaps we'll hang around for a few days, make some money, and head on back. Toby, she's my lifeline. And that little fella of hers is hers."

"You're a very handsome young man, Shawn." Of course, just like he always did, he said he knew that. Imp laughed. "What is it you do for a living, Toby? Perhaps I can look for something to help you out while you're here."

"That won't be necessary. The pot asked me to tell you that someone is coming for it." The waitress came then and took their order for their meal. After ordering her food, thinking of sharing it with Shawn, Imp asked him what he wanted. As per his usual affair, when people risked asking a six-year-old what he wanted, he told her. "Shawn, these nice people don't want to pay for a steak when they've only just met us. Just order from the menu like a good boy."

"I'm having a steak too." After it was settled that George and Shawn were going to have a steak, medium rare, Grannie changed her order to a steak too. Toby stuck with her pasta meal and tried to get back to what she'd been sent here to do. "Toby, we're going to eat first. I know you have something to tell us, and I'm very happy that you've come here to tell us. But I'd like more than anything to just relax, enjoy a good meal, and then we'll go back to our home and talk. All right?"

"Can I get me a bath?" Toby was going to find herself a deep hole and crawl to the bottom of it, hoping no one would look for her. But Imp told him that they had a really nice bathtub that he was more than welcome to use. "I have a couple of toys I play with at bath time. I didn't bring them all on account'a we're traveling light. Grannie said we had to bug out, but I was afraid that bugs were coming too, so Momma told me that we were just traveling light." He leaned over to Imp and, in his staged, very loud whisper, spoke again. "I don't know what that means either, but if Momma told me we'd be all right, I believed her."

"As you well should." She wasn't sure how it happened, but before their appetizers were brought to the table, Shawn was sitting between Imp and George, and she was enjoying her meal.

True to their word, they didn't speak of anything but the town, the things going on around town, as well as the things they'd been able to get done. Toby enjoyed herself. Grannie did as well, and when she asked if she could have a beer, Toby was almost glad they were going to the Manning home. Grannie was going to be snoring before they arrived, she'd bet.

Shawn finished his dinner before she did, but he stayed where he was. She knew he was getting sleepy. They'd not been sleeping all that well despite the large roomy seats. Not that he took a nap anymore, but he'd been cooped up for so long that she knew it was exhausting him to be upset too.

Dessert was a bowl of sherbet for Shawn, and Toby enjoyed some of it. Grannie didn't have any, but she did sample the cake that Imp had ordered. She noticed that neither of them drank coffee, and Imp drank juice. Whatever she was, Toby wasn't going to tangle with her. There was something very powerful about her.

By the time they were pulling into the Manning driveway, Toby was a nervous wreck. Grannie was sleeping, of course, and Toby was pinging off the walls again. She didn't blame him, really. To be able to be in a home and to burn off some of his never-ending energy was a good thing for everyone. As soon as they walked into the door, she backed the fuck up.

"That's a little person." Imp stood in front of her, telling her to breathe. "I can't. I can't breathe. It's a little person."

The slap to her face upset Shawn, but George was able to calm him down. When she was taken to the living room and sat on the couch, Toby looked around for more of the little creatures. Imp sat beside her and took her hand into hers.

"Will you tell me, or do I have to look?" She said she didn't like them. "It's more than that, and you know it. What happened that makes you so terrified of them? They're faeries and brownies here. Is it them, or just little people in general?"

Toby looked at the woman. "What are you? Tell me so that I know what I'm going to be dealing with when you call me a liar and toss me from your house." Imp said she was fae, but a great deal more. "I don't know what that might mean, but fae. That's what my son's father was. Not is, as I killed him, but he and his little minions kidnapped me, and he raped me over a four-day period before I was able to kill him. I might die trying to kill you, but you'll not harm me or mine."

"I wouldn't anyway. You said you killed this fae. Do you know his name?" Toby shook her head. "All right. This is Velvet. She won't touch you unless you allow it. But she's going to be—"

"I'm not lying to you." Imp told her she knew that, and she knew that her fear was genuine. "When I went to the police station after I was able to get away, they arrested me. Of course, there wasn't a body for them to find, nor was there any evidence that I'd been at the house all that time. I have a hard time holding down a job because someone will hear my name and figure out what happened to me seven years ago. Why does Velvet want to touch me?"

"She can tell who it was that did this to you. Also, she can tell you how powerful he was. In that, it'll help you be able to deal with the magic Shawn already is showing signs of." She knew they'd seen it when his glass of milk was refilled. Also, when he didn't have any catsup at the table quick enough for him to eat. "Will you allow her to do this for you?"

"I don't know what good it will do to know. I guess the magical stuff would be all right. But that's all. Nothing but a touch." Imp asked if she could touch Shawn instead if that made her feel better. "No. I don't want any of these things near my son."

"All right." When she put out her hand, Toby was ashamed that it was shaking. The little creature was very gentle with her touch, but it still made her want to scrub her hands until they were raw. She'd done that a great deal after getting away. The look on the little thing's face scared her a little. "Will she tell me too?"

"Of course. It's your right to know what sort of monster hurt you. Go on, Velvet. Tell us what you were able to find out." The little person nodded, then looked at her before she spoke. "Is it bad, Velvet? I promise you that I won't hold it against you if it is."

"Nay, my lady. 'Tis not bad. Especially knowing he is dead. I am sorry that one of my kind hurt you so grievously, my lady." She looked at Imp. "He was Ames, my lady. The nephew to the king of the fae. Ames did just as she said, but Lady Toby hasn't told the whole story to anyone just as yet. The faeries and fae that have helped Ames have been dealt with by his father. It wasn't a good death for any of them."

"How do you know this if you've only touched me? Are you reading my mind?" Velvet told her that with the name, she knew what had happened. "I'm sorry. I didn't know anyone would have cared all that much once he was dead. I didn't know he was the son of the king or whatever he was either."

"Ames has been a terrible person since he was born. His mother is said to have overindulged him greatly when he was just a child. Then one day, he was to have gone away for the murder of one of the house faeries. The king was very angry at him, as it turned out, that he'd been murdering small ones since he'd been only a babe in his crib." Imp asked where the mother was now. "She is no more, my lady. Ames took her life when she agreed with the king that Ames needed to be put away. His mind, they all agreed, was not in a good spot."

"How the hell did he get away with what he did to me?" She hadn't realized she'd yelled until the faerie backed away. "It's not your fault. I know it's not anyone else's fault, but I've been blackballed for every job I've tried to get. We've moved so many times I can't remember my address anymore. All because of that fucking prick deciding I was going to be his plaything."

"It's not you, my lady, but the boy. There are people that wish to take him from you for what he is." She said he was her son. "And the grandson of the king of the fae. He will need protection as his magic gets stronger. As it is now, it calls to the ones that wish him harm. Not only harm, Lady Toby, but they wish to bring his grandfather to heel for crimes against his son. Ames wasn't respected at all, but he was feared, and one of his last rules was to avenge his death. This was decreed long before he met and harmed you."

Not knowing what to do, she picked up Shawn when he came to her. The pajamas that he had on were like a pair he'd had at home. Holding her son tightly to her, she knew she couldn't do this on her own much longer. If she did, she was going to lose. She knew that.

"I need help." Velvet promised her that she'd have it. "While I think that's wonderful of you offering, even after the way I've treated you, I'm not sure what I can go up against magic that a king would have."

"Ah, but the king isn't after you, my lady. I will protect the three of you with my life."

The man standing in the room with her looked so much like Ames, or whatever his name was, that Toby screamed. The blackness that was coming up on her didn't just take her, but it slapped her around a couple of times before she finally was out. Whatever happened, she supposed she deserved it. That's what the cops had been telling her for years anyway.

Chapter 2

Micky, as a fae to the king—his right-hand man, as a matter of fact—had been assigned to watch over the young woman as she rested. While he knew that if he poked her, he'd get into trouble again. He had better things to do than to sit around while she lay there like she'd not been in the presence of greatness. And he wasn't talking just about himself either. But the king of all fae had come to see her, and she had the nerve to act as if he was nothing but a speck on the wall to her.

Micky had been assigned to her the day that she'd fainted dead away when she'd seen his lordship. While he knew that she'd been terrified out of her skull, a new human expression that he so loved to say, he also knew that she was quite rude for treating his lordship the way that she had. Stupid human should have been drawn and —

"If you so much as touch my momma again, I'm going to wring your neck." Micky looked at the little boy and backed away from his threat. Not that he was afraid of him, but he'd also been warned that he wasn't to do a thing with the child, or he'd be squashed. "You're looking at her all mean like I'll hurt you if you try and do anything to her. Do you hear me? I don't even know why you're here. I can watch her just fine, and I don't poke her while saying mean things to her."

The tiny creature huffed. "The entire household can hear you, young man. You should be a great deal more polite with your elders than you are. And I will do as I wish where your mother is concerned. You're much too loud and noisy to be a part of the kingdom that I am a part of. You'll need to learn your manners before someone brings it to your grandfather's attention that you're not worthy of his magic." Micky hated that he had to watch over this human and her spawn. "Why are you even claiming this human as your mother? She is unworthy of — there are much more powerful people around that you could say you're a part of. Though I'd not go telling everyone of that. There are still rules that you must follow. Keeping that mouth of your shut would be something that you should have learned long ago. I think our kind would be better off if we were just to forget that you exist and train someone else. You're much too — "

"Shut the fuck up." He looked at the woman when she spoke from beneath him. Micky glared at her, but he was, at that moment, slightly afeared of her. Once she was sitting up, flicking him away, he could see that she was somewhat pretty, but nothing like his lordship should take under his wing. "Go away. I don't know why you're here or who would have sent you but go away."

Micky puffed out his chest. "I am assigned to watch over you." She stood up, and he realized she wasn't as short in stature as he had first thought. "I take my assignments and do them to the best of my knowledge. Even if I think they are stupid as watching over something like you and this spawn of yours. I do not take orders from someone like you."

"I don't want you here, don't you get it? You leave now, and I'll not have to smash you with a book." When she reached for a book, he backed away from her. "What the fuck are you doing here anyway? To watch over me? From your words, I'm assuming that you don't care for me or my son. Not that I give a shit what you think, but I didn't ask you to be here, and as of this moment, you're not to come within a yard of me." Toby waved her had dismissively.

He felt himself being jerked from the room, sucked into a tube of smaller size. As if he were being ordered from the room where he'd been by that woman. His body was indeed squashed, and he felt sick to his tummy. Not only that, but somehow Micky was in his own home when he was able to get his bearings again. Sitting in his little rocker, he sat there for several moments thinking about what sort of power it would have taken for him to have been ordered from the room. Especially since he'd been put there by the king.

"The king has done this for me. He knew that she had awakened and sent me home. What a kind and generous man he is. Not making me sit with that human any longer than necessary." He rocked a bit more before he got up to make himself a little bit of brew. "He knew too that they'd not been the least bit nice to me either. To think that she would try and order me from the room. Like I was nothing at all. Humans. I detest them all."

Just as he was sitting down to drink his brew, he was summoned to the king. Feeling like this was going to be a wonderful time to thank him for taking him from the humans, he bowed before his lordship and smiled when he was bid to stand up. The king looked furious. Not that he blamed him. The humans were trying to take advantage of him.

"You were told to watch over the woman and her child, Toby. Why are you at home having a cup of tea when you've not been dismissed by me?" The thunder in his voice startled Micky, and he told him how the human had treated him. Or at least his version of what had happened. "So she sent you away, and you thought it fine to go home, put your feet up and have a nice rest."

"I thought that you had sent me home." He asked him why he thought that he'd do such a thing when he'd told him to do something. "I'm not sure, my lord.

She mentioned me staying away from her, and I was just sent home. She couldn't have done so without… she is only human, that creature. For all we know, she had lured Ames to her bed to make a child with him. It would not surprise me to see that is how it happened."

"So you think this young woman, a human as you're so fond of calling her, lured Ames to her bed and had him give her a child. You do understand that Ames was quite powerful in his own right, do you not? And it was never in his nature to do what anyone wished of him, especially a woman." He said that humans were a wily bunch. "I'm sure that they are. However, I'm also reasonably sure that while she might be only a human, she is a good deal smarter than you've given her credit for. How is it, Micky, that she was able to keep a magical being such as her son safe for all these years? Or a better question would be, how do you suppose she was able to keep me from finding out about him? I'd say that, even with her wily ways, as you called them, there is no reason to believe that she was capable of making Ames do anything that he didn't wish. In fact, I do believe her when she tells me that he raped her over and over then she had to kill him. From what I'm hearing, it should have happened to him long ago."

Micky took a couple of steps back in horrified shock. "She killed him?" His lordship said nothing but did stare at him until Micky felt uncomfortable. "I shall go back to the woman posthaste, my lord. I will keep an eye on her for you and make sure that she does nothing to harm you or our kind. I will make sure too that she is given the rules in which she must follow concerning you and our kind."

"No. I think, and I'm sure this is about right, that even should you want to go back to her, you'd not be able to go anywhere near her or the little boy, Shawn. She has, in some way, banned you from coming near her. I can see the traces of magic that she may well have used. Or her son had." He said that he doubted that a human like her could do such a thing. "Be that as it may, you'll keep your distance from her and her son. I don't wish to have to tell you how much they mean to me."

"They're only human, sire. What on earth are you thinking? Aligning yourself with someone like that isn't something that you should be doing. Why, you'd be better off just ignoring them and going on with your life." The king stood up, and Micky felt it all the way to his bones, the anger coming off the man. "You see that I am right then. I'm glad that you summoned me, my lord. This could have been a disaster. However, I was just thinking. You should have them killed off, the two of them. That way, they won't be able to come back on you—if you would allow it, my lord, I'll take care of that right away for you. What do you think?"

Micky was proud of himself for that last idea. If they were both dead and forgotten, there would be no more assignments for him to be watching over them. It was bad enough that the woman had told any and all that would listen that she was 'supposedly' raped by young Ames. Micky had liked the young prince fae and was saddened that he'd not be able to work with him when he took over the kingdom someday. Micky looked up when the great king growled

"You dare council me? On my own family?" Micky felt his body stiffen in pain. His lordship was hurting him, and he didn't understand why. "You dare to tell me how I should feel? How I should be treating these people that have never asked me for a thing? Micky, fae of my kingdom, you are no longer welcome in my realm. You will no longer have a place in my mind. As of this moment, you are banished to spend your days with the humans until such time as you—"

"Stop this right now. You can't do that to me." He knew his mistake the moment that he spoke. "I mean, you could, your lordship, but why would you want to banish me? I've done nothing wrong. I've only been doing as you told me to do."

"You are banished. Forevermore." The snap of something touching his skin made him cry out. Micky wasn't sure what was going on. Surely the king didn't really mean what he was saying and held his head as he was once again sucked through space and time to someplace he didn't know where it was.

Micky found himself with his things sitting on a tree branch that had nary a leaf on it to shade him from the sun. Not only that but his teacup and pot were busted beyond repair. As he was gathering up his pitiful amount of things, things that had been in his lovely home when he'd been there earlier, he was nearly crushed by a beast of an animal that was sniffing him when he went to pick up his broken lid from the ground.

The dog, he realized what it was, was wearing a collar that was bright blue and had a name on it. Micky no more cared what its name was than he did most things to do with beasts. But when a man reached down to touch the dog with his hand, he stopped moving. Well, he didn't actually stop moving but vibrated more than he thought was necessary.

"You must be Micky. I was told to look for you. My name is Ignis." He asked him if he was going to be housing him. "Housing? I suppose you could call it that. I'm here raising cattle for the area. You can bunk in there with the rest of the fae."

"Rest of the fae? Are you insane? I'm the right-hand man to the king. I will be bunking, as you called it, in the house where the other royals stay." He moved away from his belongings. "Take those to the house, Ignis. I would expect you to have me in the best room with the best sunlight coming through. And I will not be sharing a room with anyone else. As I said, I'm the right-hand man to the king of all fae."

The man did pick up his things and put them

into his pocket. This was more like it. It was less than he wanted, but it was still better than he'd hoped for from a mere human. When the man also picked him up, putting him on the back of the dog, Micky was startled. Asking him what the meaning of this was, the man laughed harder. It wasn't until they were standing in front of a great smelly building that Micky decided that this joke or whatever it was had gone far enough.

"What do you think you're about? This is no way to treat me." Ignis turned and looked at him without saying a word. Taking him off the smelly beast, he told someone by the name of Mr. Trouble to go into the house. It was only him and the man standing there staring at one another as the dog had bounced off. "Well? What do you think is going to happen now?"

"We're up at five around here to start out the day. The cows are milked at that time. You'll have to get with the supervisor tonight to see what part of the job you're going to be—" He cut him off, saying that he didn't work with cows. Whatever they were needing from him would need to be done by someone else. "You'll do as you're told. And you'll do it now. According to King Andar, a friend of the family, you're to be set to work with the cows for punishment. While I know what you did to piss him off, I don't care enough to get into it with you as to why you think that whatever you have to say means shit to me. You get out of hand, and I'm to call my sister. Imp will take care of you if you give her any shit."

"This is outrageous." The man walked away. "I'll not be subject to this sort of treatment. I hate all humans, and I will not tolerate being treated thusly. See that I don't report you to the king as soon as he regains his senses over that stupid human and her child. You'll see who makes the rules and who follows them.

Ignis turned to him and seemed to grow in power. Showing his true self, flame and fire, Micky jumped back so quickly that he hit his head on the boards behind him. As flames began to dance around his wings, Micky pulled them into himself, fearful that he was going to be burnt alive here and waited for this nightmare to end.

"You'll do as you're told." When he walked away this time, Micky held his tongue. There was no way that the king, his king, would do this to someone like him. In the morning, he was going to make plans to figure out when he was returning to his own place.

Looking at his mess of belongings, there was very little that wasn't soiled or broken. Talking to himself as he gathered his things up, he looked around for a place where he could sleep this evening. Getting to the bottom of all this was going to take a great deal of time. However, he thought that once he was finished, there would be heads rolling that—

Micky looked to where the man had gone. The flames. The name, what was it meant by his name? Both words nudged at his mind as if he should know it. But thinking about what was there, knowing actually that the rumors had to be false, he decided that it was just that. A myth. A myth that three faes, a family, had made the dragons and their breaths. His king was being modest. Hiding under a shadow so that no one knew his greatness. There was no way that the rest of the myth was even close to being true.

"Surely they did not create the world as we know it. Especially not that man there as a part of it. He's as dumb as a post." Micky shoved his personal belongings under the straw-like things that were strewn about the floor. "There is no way that a being as powerful—

supposedly more powerful than my king could have created anything like the dragon. Stupid human." Still, he had turned to flames. His name was Ignis. "It's just unbelievable the things that people would do or say in the name of trying to look to be more than they really were."

~*~

Toby needed to get out of the house. The people there were extremely nice to let them stay there, but she needed to get home and get someplace to live with her little family. A job too. She needed that more than anything. Perhaps now that she'd done what the teapot had told her — tell the man named George Manning that someone was coming after the pot, she'd be rewarded. While she didn't do it solely for the money, giving him the warning, it would be helpful to be able to find a job and not have to stress about everything else that came with being homeless and unemployed.

After telling the cook that she and Shawn were going to go to Coshocton for a few hours, she was given a list of things that the two of them could do while there. All of it, she was told, was free to them if she handed the small token to the front desk. The

Mannings were good friends with the village.

Toby was glad for that. With the little bit of money that she'd stashed away, she and Shawn could pick up a few things to marvel over later when they were back home and have some lunch. They'd not had a single day where they could have leisured over a lunch since the teapot had contacted her.

It had been in the storage shed when she'd realized that it wasn't in her mind that someone was calling for her. Finding the beautiful green teapot wrapped in the dirty newspaper had made her happy. Then it started telling her what she needed to do.

It had taken her two days to find the cheapest and ugliest clay to wrap around the pot. Then another day of it drying out so that it would be hard around it. She'd nearly been caught when her uncle had come into the house with some equally ugly pots from the shed.

"Where did that come from?" She told him that she'd picked it up at a garage sale. "That's not going to stay in my house. I'll take it to the auction house to get rid of it for you. If I get more than a nickel for it, then I'm keeping it."

The teapot had told her that was perfect. She could contact someone named George to purchase it so that it would get to the rightful owner. The teapot, she'd said her name was Ava, said that since she'd been so kind to her, she'd make sure that she was rewarded for her time and help.

"Mom?" Toby was just pulling into a parking space when Shawn turned to her. "Do you think that the reward will be something like money or maybe just another stupid teapot? I mean, you don't even like tea. But money, as grannie says, makes the world go around."

"Yes, money would be nice. But whatever it is, we'll be grateful for it. We helped some people out and also, hopefully, got it to the person that Uncle Donald had stolen it from." Shawn knew all about her uncle and father. "How about we don't think about what we might get and take some time today to just pretend like we haven't a care in the world."

"I'd like that." The first thing they did was go to the office of the village. The token had done just what the cook had said it would and got them free armbands for the little working shops. She was also given a gift card. It had been from Imp and George to have lunch on them.

Toby had no idea what to expect when she was told that the card was for five hundred dollars but decided right then and there she was going to spend every penny of it on Shawn today to give him a day of it. If they'd not been meant to spend it all, then she'd figure out a way for her to pay them back. Today was for the two of them.

The first thing that the two of them did was to scope out the shops and stores. There were a great many of them, but she and Shawn thought that they'd enjoy the General Store most of all. As they started their tours of the working buildings, Toby kept an eye on Shawn.

He wasn't one to wander off. Since he'd been a baby, he somehow knew that he could only trust her and Grannie. Never once in school had he spent the night with anyone. He had never wanted sleepovers at their house or birthday parties. She would gladly have done any of those things had he only asked.

Instead of having a nice lunch, they decided to have sandwiches made at the Mercantile. They had ready to eat sandwiches as well as a variety of drinks that she'd never heard of. Getting a bag of chips for each of them, she was standing in line when she realized that Shawn was staring out the window. Leaning down to him, she asked him what was going on.

"I'm not sure." She didn't question him more but did what she'd done when she'd been told about it at the house. To reach out to someone, anyone that was a Manning. "Mom, I think we're going to need some help. Can you call someone?" She told him she was doing that right now. When he gripped her hand tighter, she was terrified out of her mind.

"Hello?" She was startled by the male voice and his apparent humor. "I don't believe I've met you, so I'm assuming that you're—I can feel your fear. Can you tell me who you are and what is going on?"

"I don't know. My son...he's with me. He's asked me to find a Manning to help us. We're in the Mercantile in Coshocton. Do you know where that is?" He said that he was in the area right now, picking up things from the bakery. "Can you...I don't know. Somehow connect to him so that he can talk to you about it? I'm standing here waiting for our food to be ready to go — I'm nervous."

"You're doing fine. Is your son touching you? The male child that I feel near you?" She said his name was Shawn. "All right, Shawn, tell me what it is you're feeling? My name is Dover, by the way."

"We're being followed. But it's not a good feeling like someone is just watching over us to protect us. I can feel that he wants to separate me from my mom. And he's not good in his heart." He asked him if he could point him out to his mother. "No. That's what has me feeling weird. He's only in the reflections, like glass or shadows. I saw it on a movie once where this man could blend himself away from people, but he couldn't hide his reflection or shadow. But they never saw that part until the end of the movie, of course."

"All right, Shawn, that's incredibly helpful for me. I want you to stick to your mother. My brother George just joined me and Winnie. I think that you know both of them." He said that he did. Toby asked if they'd be all right. "Yes, so long as you do what I ask of you. I don't want either of you harmed, but I don't want this guy to be able to follow you around, either."

"I like that idea. I don't need any more strife

in my life." He told her that he was coming into the restaurant now. He joined her in the que for food. "I'm Toby Deavers."

"I've heard about you." When he leaned toward her and kissed her neck, she thought that she would surely die from the sensations. "Pretend that we know each other. That way, it will throw the person off if he's been sent to find only a woman and boy."

Since their sandwiches were just about finished up, Dover ordered some food for himself. The people behind the line had been really nice to them before Dover showed up, but they were practically falling all over each other to get his food order. The owner came out and hugged him.

Toby had never felt such violent rage as she did at the moment. Not for anything. But the moment the elderly lady put her arms around Dover, Toby wanted to rip her eyes out and tear her beating heart from her chest. It was all she could do to bring in enough breath.

"I have you." Nodding, she told Dover that she was fine. "No, you're not. I'm not going to leave you. Mrs. Mckenna is a good friend of mine. Nothing more."

She would have scoffed off the idea that she

needed Dover to say that to her, but it did calm her a great deal. As the three of them stood there, waiting for his sub, she looked around at the store. Anything to keep her mind off of the jealous rage that had consumed her.

The shop was filled with all sorts of treasures, she guessed that one would call them. Along with the meat counter, there were packaged cheeses, bags of cheese and sausage to carry around. And every kind of salsa a person would ever want to try. Flavored popcorns. Things with the name of the town on them, as well as shirts and sweatshirts. There was even an ice cream shop in the back. Toby looked at Dover when he said her name.

"Are you ready?" She smiled at him as he handed her the picnic basket. She asked him what it was. "Mrs. Mckenna found out that you and I are going to go down by the lake to eat, and she fixed us up."

She was headed to the door, ashamed of herself, when she was stopped going out first. Dover moved around the two of them to block their path. Kneeling down to Shawn, he asked her son if he could see the man. Toby looked at the building across the street before answering.

"He's just beside the sign that says bags. When I look at him from this distance, he's blurry. But when I'm closer, like he was when we came in here, he looked like an invisible man." Dover didn't move but to stand. When he smiled at her, she wondered what was going on. "Mr. Dover, he's scary big. And sometimes, when he's very close to us, I can see that he has a sword in his hand."

"You're wonderfully observant, Shawn. Just one more second here, and we'll be free for the rest of the afternoon." She watched Shawn interact with the man. Toby knew the exact moment that something had happened across the street. "He's been taken care of, son. You know that was the only way, correct?"

"Yes, sir. As my grannie says, better him than me." After tousling his hair, they left the store. "Mom, if I eat all my lunch, can we come back here for an ice cream."

"Yes. Anything you want. You saved us today, baby. I'm so glad that we did this, but I'm sorry it was marred by that man." Dover said it hadn't been a man and that he would explain it later. She was in a fog as they made their way to the picnic area just down the street from the store.

The food was fantastic. While she'd not been paying attention, other things had been added to their food. Inside the picnic basket, she not only found a beautiful blanket that they used as a table cloth, but there were utensils, small tubs of salads, as well as cheese and crackers to enjoy. There was also a variety of the sodas that she'd looked at too.

Gingham painted plates and napkins, as well as wine glasses, was in the basket as well. Toby felt touched by the gesture and felt horrible about her earlier feeling toward the woman. It wasn't until George and Winnie joined them that they spoke about what had happened. George asked Winnie if she'd killed the thing by removing his head.

"I destroyed him. Not just killed. Things like that have to have their head removed in order to know that they won't be able to come back and try again. It's what I was created for, to protect." The other two had food, but it didn't look like anything from the store. Winnie shared the faerie salad, mostly greens with fruit in it, with her. It was delicious. "The man had been hired by a human to hunt the two of you down. With the magic that he had, he might well have been able to get away with it, too, had Shawn not been able to see him. Without, it might have been days after he'd taken you to realize what had happened."

"Should we expect this to happen all the time? The reason that I ask is I need to get home. Shawn starts school soon, and I need to get a job." Winnie asked her why she didn't just stay here. So that they could protect them. "I can't ask you to protect us. We only came here to warn George of someone coming after the teapot. We did that, and now we've got to return home."

"She promised us a reward too." Shawn smiled at her before continuing. "We don't know what it is or anything. Mom said she'd help before the teapot told her about that part. Whatever it is, we're going to love it because it was nice of the teapot to do. Right, mom?"

"Yes, that's right." Dover started laughing. As he sat there, nearly choking to death on his salad George started pounding him on the back. Twice Dover looked over at her and laughed all the harder. "What is the matter with you? Have you gone insane or something. Straighten up and act right. What is wrong with you?"

"I'd say that you've gotten your reward. Perhaps nothing you were expecting, I think. I know that's what I'm going to consider it. For myself and my family." She asked him what he was going on about. George asked him if he was sure. "I'm so very sure." Dover looked over at her. "I'm so sorry for laughing, Toby. I truly am. But the teapot somehow knew that the two of us were mates. I belong to you."

She looked at Winnie and George, and they both smiled at her. "I can't be a mate to someone like you." Dover cocked a brow at her. "Not that I think there is anything wrong with you. You seem perfect. But I'm just a person. A human as that creature Micky was fond of telling me. But I'm not mate material. Not in your world."

"Because I'm a dragon?" She told him that was part of it. "What's the rest? I'm thinking it might be that you're a human part? That doesn't bother me at all. Is it to do with Shawn? It shouldn't. I will raise him to be of my blood like any child you'd like to have with me if we get to that point. Or is it the money?"

"You have a great deal of it." He nodded and said that she did, too, now. "No. I don't want you to think of me as a charity case. I'm well capable of taking care of myself. And my son."

"I'm positive that you are capable of taking care of a great many things. I won't ever tell you that you can't do something. However, I would hope that if you needed help, you'd not hesitate to ask for it. Wait, you have already done that, haven't you?" She said she wasn't stupid either. "I would never have thought that you were. You, just for reference, deferred to me when you realized you were in over your head with the fae. You didn't hesitate at all to believe your son or not when he told you that you needed help. Nor did you, and I'm so very proud of you for this not buckle under the pressure of others keeping you out of harm's way. You did exactly what you needed to do to get yourself safe and sound."

"I don't have anything but my family." He said that if she would allow it, she'd have more than that. "I'm not saying that this will work out with us. But my family, my son and Grannie come first to me in everything."

"As they should. And you, with them, will be a priority to me over everyone else when you need me. And my family will do the same should you need them as well." She said that she'd not expect that from anyone. "No. You'd not. But as of the moment that I acknowledged you as my mate, not even if I'd not touched you, you received a great deal of magic. More than you had before."

"I had magic before?" He only nodded a look at Shawn. "Because of his father, you mean. I didn't ask for that either."

"If he weren't already dead, my dear, I would find him right now and tear him into such small pieces that they'd never be able to put him back together. Then I would set fire to the area where he died so that anyone sniffing around for him would know that he was killed by a powerful dragon." Dover smiled at her. "However, I think it's better if people know that a powerful dragon's mate killed a fae prince to save herself for me."

The rest of the meal was talking about anything and everything else. Shawn was peppering them all with questions about what they were and where they'd live if she would agree. Tuning him out and the others, Toby realized that she'd been feeling less stressed since

Dover had joined them. She felt...well, loved wasn't the name she'd give to the things she was feeling, but it was nice to be able to depend on someone else, even if it was only for a few minutes.

Getting ice cream was about all she could take today. She had a great deal on her mind, but she was determined to not let any of it spoil her day with Shawn. Dover asked if he could join them, and before she was going to tell him—well, she wasn't sure what she was going to tell him. Shawn said that it would be great.

It was, she realized, when they were headed back to George's home. He'd not been pushy at all about anything. While she knew that he was keeping an eye out for danger, he never let on that he was afraid or bored with the two of them. While driving back in her own car, Shawn talked about all the things that they'd done. She supposed that he was starved for male company the way he went on about having Dover around. But it had been a blast.

Chapter 3

Dover was ecstatic. While Toby was a bit quiet right now, he knew that she was quite capable of letting him know when she needed something. Not that she'd been rude, but she had been upset about him telling her that she could stay in his home with her family for as long as she wished.

"I'm not going to leap into bed with you simply because you have this macho shit going on with me being your mate." He dared not laugh, but it was hard not to. He explained what he meant. "Oh. I'm sorry, then. I thought...well, I guess I made it clear what I thought you meant. I'm not used to this. People are usually nice to you right up until they stab you in the back, but you're just too nice all the time. Not that that's not a good thing. I'm just not used to it."

"The house is yours to do with whatever you wish. I have been adding things to it as I come across it. Things here and there that I've come across when out with my family. The bunk bed set in the bedroom that we looked in earlier wasn't there when I left. I'm thinking that Ignis or one of his sisters put it in there when they found out that you have a son to share with me." She asked how that happened. "Magic. I'm sure, too, that if you were to ask him, he made it special for Shawn. Like he has for the other children in the family. My older brother, Finn, and the others have been cleaning out some of the old barns around here that were purchased with the houses. Also, the buildings downtown have been cleared out that we've purchased as well. Not usually a lot of stuff in there but some smaller items. There was also some stuff that was brought here by my parents when they moved here. If you'd like to head over there sometime, we can find other things to fill out the house. One of the things that I don't have is a table and chairs for the dining room yet. I haven't any idea what should be in there at this point. And since until today it was just me here, I didn't bother overly much."

"Oak." He agreed with her immediately. Dover was happy too that she seemed to like the natural woods of the little bit of furniture that he had already. But in a heartbeat, he would have changed it out for her if she hadn't. "I have a few things in storage. Not a great amount. When we came here to talk to George, we were already behind in our rent. I was terrified that the landlord would sell it off when he realized that we were gone. I'd like to bring that here. If you'd not mind."

"I don't mind at all. I'm to understand that you left in the middle of the night. Shawn said that you bugged out." She laughed, telling him the memory of him trying to figure out why they were getting up in the middle of the night and having to leave a lot of his things behind. "He's a smart kid, that one. He told me that he knew that you were having a hard time with things. The only thing that he was going to miss was his yard, as it had a swing in it. I'm sure that we can have him a swing up in no time."

"The faeries." He nodded. Dover watched her shiver. "They seem to be following us around all the time. I'm assuming that they'll get things finished up faster than a person could."

"Yes. They want to please you. They've been around me my entire life. They're hoping that you'll shake things up a bit for them." She moved into the kitchen, and he quickly explained that it was going to be renovated starting next week. "I've been trying to get my head together about the foundation that we've started here with the Manning money. The house took second in that. But now that you're here, I think it'll be easier to get everything the way that it needs to be. At some point, I'm sure that we're going to have to go into town and get some things for the household. Such as linens and plates. Again, since it was just me, I only had the single plate and fork, and if I needed a spoon for something, I'd just drink it out of my bowl."

She looked at him then. Her face scrunched up in seriousness. "I'm terrified of the little people. I know that, in a way, they were doing what they were told, but there were a few that seemed to be enjoying torturing me. One of them, in particular, would take my food and pee on it. My water would be dumped. Ames knew about it too. He thought it was a 'lark' he called it." He asked her if she remembered their names, that someone would take care that they were punished. "I'm sorry, but I don't believe that anyone will. He was the king's next in line. And they seemed to be doing just exactly what he wanted them to do at all times. Make me suffer at his hands."

"There were others that he did the same thing to." She said that she knew that. And that he'd killed them too. "Was that what was happening when you were able to kill him? He was ready to end what he had going on with you?"

"Yes. He told me that he was finished with me. At first, I was so happy that I was going to die. That, perhaps, the suffering would end for me. You understand?" He nodded. "Then he told me that he had already found himself someone else to take my place in his bed. A woman of quality that didn't fight him at every turn. I hadn't any idea what he meant by quality, but something surged up in me, and it was all I could do not to scream. Almost as soon as he touched me, I knew an anger that hadn't touched me before. So somehow, I fought him off."

"How did you manage to kill him? I'm assuming that the faeries were helping him if they were there." She told him that he'd sent them on ahead of him, taking care that the next woman was ready for him. "I'm so sorry that you had to do that. To defend yourself against someone so evil. It should never have happened to you."

"I was surprised myself that I was able to pull it off. Killing him, I mean. It seemed that every time that I hurt him, he'd heal before I could make another blow to his body. Then, just like that, something popped into my head, and I knew that if I were able to remove his head, then he'd be dead. I didn't know that before. But once I knocked him out, I took his head off." He asked her if he'd had a knife. "Oh yes. A beautiful one. Would you like to see it?"

Before he could imagine where she might have it, she simply reached into the air, and it filled her hand. The magic, so much of it that he stepped back from her hand, seemed to make it glow. Asking first if he could touch it, she nodded but told him to be extra careful that it didn't seem to like to be touched by anyone but her.

"I wasn't going to take it with me when I left, but then I thought of fingerprints. As I was trying to think of a way to clean myself and it up, it stood up and spoke to me. I haven't any idea what it said to me, but I did get the idea that it was going to be with me when I needed it." The blade allowed him to touch it, then to pick it up. While no eyes appeared on it, Dover could feel it looking at him. Perhaps even study him a bit. "I hadn't any idea what I looked like after killing Ames. I do know that he'd gotten in a few punches of his own, as well as this knife cutting into me. I was also starved and dehydrated too. After the knife disappeared and then reappeared in my hand a couple of times, I got that I could call it if I needed it. Exhaustion or something dragged me to the floor of the cave, and I slept. Or passed out. When I woke up, not only was Ames gone, but all my cuts and wounds were healed up. There was also a note with a set of clothing for me to wear. I still have the note. I don't know what it says either."

"I'm thinking that it's in fae. As for his body, I can only assume that the faeries took it while you slept and buried it someplace. His faeries would have done that for him. Other faeries would have left him there to rot." Handing her back the blade, he looked just behind her. "You do know that he's dead. I mean, you killed him so that anyone that might look like him wouldn't be him."

"He's back, isn't he? The father or whatever he was to Ames is back." He nodded. When Toby turned slowly, he wrapped his hands around her to keep her safe. Not that he thought that Andar would harm her, but he was a being that he'd had very little to do with since he'd been around. "Andar, this is my mate, Toby Deaver Manning. She survived the kidnapping and killing of Ames when he took her from her home."

"She has a son by him. The only living child of him." There was a hardness to his voice, and it wasn't until Winnie, protector of the Dragons, stood beside him that he realized how stupid he'd been not to call someone in when the blade had appeared. "I wish no harm to come to either of them, my lady Winnie. I am only here so that I might take the boy back with me to train him in ways that he will be able—"

"You will not take my son anyplace. He's mine."

Andar looked at him, pleading in his eyes. "He's not going to let you either. At least he'd better not. Shawn is my son, and I fought a long hard war to keep him, and you'll leave us the fuck alone."

"Surely you jest. He's royalty. You may visit him from time to time. I won't be cruel and keep you from him." Toby told him that it wasn't going to be an issue because Shawn wasn't going with him. Andar looked at him. "Dover. You have to make her see reason. If she doesn't allow me to take him with me so that I can train him, then it will be too late. He'll be like…well, he'll be too much like her, and that wouldn't work out for the kingdom."

"Fuck your kingdom." Winnie stood in front of Andar when he took a step toward Toby. While she'd not pulled her blade out, she was about as ready as she could be. Toby stepped around Winnie to confront the king of all fae. "Fuck you too. Did you know what a monster he was? Did you do a damned thing to make sure that he didn't hurt others? I doubt that. I doubt it so much that I hold you just as responsible for what he did to those other women as he did me."

"That is enough." Ames took a step toward Toby

when suddenly the room tightened, and he felt rather than saw his family behind them. Not just his brothers but his father, uncles and their sons as well. All dragons ready to defend his mate should she need it. However, he wasn't so sure that she did. "You dare to threaten me with dragons? I will destroy you all should you—"

Ignis appeared first. He had loved this man since he joined the family some weeks ago. He just smiled at them all and sat down on the floor beside Toby's feet with his legs crossed at the ankles. Then Glacier appeared. She had with her a stool that she sat on, and then she turned and offered the men behind her a cookie from her tin. All partook of them, even he did. Then the room brightened so much that he was sure that they'd be burnt from the glow of it.

"Hello, Andar." Imp, just as her name implied, hopped around the room, telling the others there that she was so glad that they'd been able to make it. When she turned back to Andar, she held out a faerie that was in chains. "This is Micky. I'm sure you know him. He was paired with your son, Ames. You should ask me why I have him in chains right now." Andar didn't move. "Ask me."

The command in her voice was stronger than he'd ever heard, even his uncle, the king of dragons, use with compulsion. When he looked at the fae king, he could see the blood running from his eyes, and his ears seemed to have sprouted a leak as well. Finally, he did as she commanded him.

"Thank you so much for asking." She held out Micky again. "He was working for you, he told me. Micky was on the hunt for someone to kill off my new sister and her son, by your command, no less. So that you'd not be bothered with them. Is that why you want to take the boy with you, Andar? If it is, I'm going to end you right now. I'm not shitting with you right now."

"I said no such thing to him." Micky screamed that Andar had. "I did not. Micky told me of his plan, and I sent him away to be with humans. I would... he was with the cattle. I thought there was a no more deserving place for him to be but with cows that eat and poop all day."

"I did receive a message from someone that I was to keep the fae busy. I never thought beyond having him find the one in charge of the barn to keep him busy the other day. That is entirely my fault for not looking deeper into it." Ignis smiled up at him. "I apologize from the bottom of my heart, dear brother. Had I known what he was up to, I would have destroyed him myself."

The faeries that were in the room came to stand with Imp. Toby backed up closer to him, but then she separated herself a little to stand by Imp, who was still holding Micky. He didn't know what she was thinking, but he felt that it wasn't going to bode well for either Micky nor Andar if things didn't smooth out soon.

"You tried to murder me." Micky spit at her. "Such a monster for one so small. You do know that in your current situation, I could easily murder you."

"You try, and my king will avenge my death immediately. You should have died when my lord said he was finished with you. As did all the others." She asked him if he'd known about the others all along. "Of course I did. I helped Lord Ames get the women by slipping things into their food and drinks. I was paired to him to be his helper in all ways. The king himself decreed it so."

Everyone looked at the king. "I had no idea. I

didn't decree for him to help in the savagery of women. I swear it on my life that I didn't know this was going on." Micky lifted his chin up when Toby turned back to him. "He is as much a monster as my son was. Just as his father was. Ames wasn't my child. When my own mate was murdered, my brother came to me and offered me his son. His eldest. In desperation, I took him under my—" Andar looked at Micky. "He killed my mate, didn't he? Ames killed my mate so that he would be given to me as my next in line?"

"I killed her when it was clear that the two of you weren't going to be anything helpful to your brother's son. Ames was just a child, and you barely took notice of him. Then he was given to you, and it was as if he were reborn. A wonderful person couldn't have been born to either of you and that mate of yours. Once Ames and I were together, it was easy for us to do things that would make him a much better king than you ever were. Your sick, pathetic ways of running the kingdom were making us ill." It was Toby that asked why he'd said that he was loyal to him when it was obvious that he wasn't. "I did what was necessary to rid the world of whoever was in my way. And that would have been you—still will be you before I am finished."

Winnie only moved. That was all it took for her to destroy the fae. She was the protector of dragons, and as such, she protected his mate and son today. When she bowed before the dragons, she turned her attention to Andar. He looked like a broken man.

~*~

Toby was on the back deck when Cindi, Dover's mother, joined her. She'd been out here a while. Just thinking about what had happened in the house. Looking over at the beautiful woman, she decided that she needed to talk more than she wanted to listen.

"Several days before I was taken from my home, I was promoted at my job. It wasn't a great job, but the money was good, and it kept my Grannie and I with food in the house. My father, Daniel, was in prison. I think he was in for the second time since I was born. He's a career criminal. I guess he'd be called. Anyway. My uncle, Donald, he was quickly working his way up to be neck and neck with my father to be most wanted." Cindi asked if she wanted some tea. "No. I don't care for it. But I'd love a glass of juice. I'm assuming that you're not going to leave me but make it."

"The faeries are going to bring it out. I'd like for you to be around them a little at a time. I understand completely why you have no trust in them. But they'd die before harming any of us." The juice and some still steaming scones were put on the little table that hadn't been there before. "So this job, what was it you did for a living?"

"Teacher. First grade. I loved the kids, don't get me wrong, but there wasn't enough money for me to support myself and be the teacher that I wanted to be. I began to understand why teachers don't make it past the first few years. Some spend more than they make in those first few years by getting all the supplies that they might need in order to do a good job of teaching. And the kids, not all but some of them, are raised to be so entitled that it's difficult to work with their parents on setting them up for success." Cindi sipped her tea and said that was what she'd discovered recently. "Anyway, I'd been promoted to be the assistant to the principal. It wasn't until a few days later that I discovered that it didn't give me any more money, and I was expected to teach my class too. It was just too much for me."

She looked out over the expanse of the back yard that was Dover's. He'd told her last night that the house and all his accounts now had her name on them. Then this morning, he'd left her a stack of cash, thousands of dollars, to go and buy things at an auction that was happening tonight. Toby looked over at Cindi.

"I have an assignment for this evening while Dover and his brother, Hedley, are gone. I hope you'll come with me. It's an auction." Cindi told her that the others were going too. "Oh, goody. I can make a fool of myself in front of everyone."

They both laughed. "Go on and finish your story. I want to hear it. I know a bit about you and your family. We'd never take the chance of letting someone hurt you, and that would include your father and uncle. You should also be aware that Donald will be released soon. Some kind of technicality that is setting him free."

"I was told this morning. Thank you." She watched the faeries as they flew around the flowers and buds. "Had I not called off sick that day and been home, I shudder to think what might have happened to my grannie. Ames or Micky would have killed her to get me to go with them. As it was, she was at her doctor's appointment, and I was in the yard messing around with the mint that someone thought it a bright idea to plant next to the house. Everywhere you stepped, it smelled like a mint factory."

"We had the same trouble years ago. I think that the faeries thought it a wonderful smell, in smaller quantities. However, with all of us tramping through it, it was just too much even for them. I think it took them a week to get it under control." Cindi sat her cup down and looked at her. "He would have killed her. You know that, don't you? From what we're finding out about Ames and the women, and there are hundreds of them, he would kill entire families to get to the woman that he wanted without thought to age or anything else. I'm sure you're glad that she wasn't there."

"I am. Everyday. She's my rock." Twisting around in the chair, she looked at her future mother-in-law. "I've been thinking about a lot of things while I've been out here. It's calming, I guess, to know that I'm safe. But the book that you gave me, it's been very helpful too. You came out here to tell me something else. What is it? And just so we're clear, I'd like for you to know that I want you to come to me when you have something to say or teach me. I don't want us to be like a lot of families."

"Never. And I won't try to teach you anything, Toby, unless you wish it. I'd like to think that I'm a good mother-in-law that doesn't intrude. Not that I don't want to, but I'm going to give it my best shot." Again, they both laughed. "Yes, I did have a few things that I wanted to tell you. First of all, and I'm so happy about this, but you and Dover can have a child together. However, it will only be the one time. Him being a dragon and you not one, it's dangerous for you to be able to carry such a beast. A boon was given to all of my sons to have a child of their own. You can or not adopt as many or as few as you wish. But you'll only have the one child by Dover." Nodding, she wondered what it would be like to have a child with a partner around. "The next thing is, you're immortal. A true immortal. Nothing can kill you. Well, Imp can, I suppose. She created dragons. But you won't ever be ill again. Nor will Shawn or your Grannie. Did you know that she had cancer?"

"Yes. She only had a few months to live, they said. But I have noticed that she seemed to be getting around a good deal better since moving in here." Nodding, Cindi said that she would continue to do so. "Okay, cut the shit and tell me whatever it is that brought you out here. You didn't just come here to tell me that I'm immortal and that I won't get sick."

"I want you to know first of all that I had nothing to do with this. It was done before you came here. And the rest of the magic came to you when you were acknowledged by Andar." She asked her what she was talking about. "Just the messenger. You're fae. Almost as much as a true-born fae. When you were being rapped by Ames, he essentially gave you some of himself. Each time. Magic. We think that is the reason that you were able to survive enough to kill him. Then when Andar figured out about Ames and what he'd done to you, he granted you all the magic that was his. Including your son and Grannie got some of the magic as well." She asked her what that meant. "That, and again, I'm just telling you this, I don't know a lot of details, but you can fly."

"I'm sorry. What did you say?" Cindi laughed.

It was a beautiful sound and repeated what she'd said. "Fly as in having wings? That sort of flying?"

"I'm not entirely sure what other way that you'd be able to fly but yes, with wings and such. Also, and this one is very important, you are now the helpmate to Andar and all the fae. His daughter-in-law, as it so happens." Toby wasn't sure that was right. She hated his son and said as much to Cindi. "Be that as it may, he has let his kingdom know that you are his breath and ruler. I don't know what that means in terms of you ruling, but you have a great deal of magic coming from that."

"And if I have sex with Dover, there will be more." Cindi nodded. Toby looked at the yard again. "I'm not against having sex with him. I know you're his mother but having sex with him isn't scary. Nor does he frighten me. I've had sex too since Ames, so I know that I'm not repugnant of it."

"I should hope not." Cindi laughed again, that hardy laugh that still had the sound of bells. "I want you to be able to come to me when you need to, Toby. I know that you've been very generous with Shawn in hanging out with my husband and the others. I think they're having a wonderful time. He's a delightful little boy."

"When I first came out here, all I could think about was the things that I was going to have to do to live here. Getting him enrolled in school. Finding a doctor for us. Making sure that he gets some of the things that were at our old home. Pay the back rent — you get it. Then I thought of the other women that were here already. How they must have had the same list. And just like that, the stress of it just floated away." Cindi said that she was glad that she was thinking along those lines. "I'm not saying that I'm not still nervous about things, but I think I have a much better handle on things than I did when I first came here."

"And you'll get better at it as you live around here. We're all into projects that help the community. There is a shelter for women who are just out of prison. To give them a heads up. I was just thinking that you might be able to help them with a few skills to get them going in the world. Like a few of them can't read or write." Toby told her that she'd gladly do anything that they needed. "Just remember to say no if you have too much on your plate, Toby. We don't want anyone to be stressed."

"I have learned to say no. Trust me." Toby thought of the woman sitting across from her. "I'm not sure what I can contribute to this family. Other than helping out. I have no money. In fact, I'm in the red most of the time. I don't have a job anymore. All I have is what you see. You can take it or leave it. However, I want you to know that I do like you and Xavier. And think that you did a wonderful job raising your sons. All of them. They've been nothing but polite and nice to me. I'm terrified of the women, including you. And Winnie makes me think that she'd eyeing me up for something. But other than that, I'd love to be a part of this family."

"You already are." Cindi stood up, and Toby did as well. "I've also been sent here to distract you a bit. So that the faeries can get into your head and find out what you wish in a home. They've also brought your things here. All of it from the other apartment. It's now in the rooms that they belong in. They've also taken care that my newest grandson has all he needs to be happy. More than anything, they want you all to be happy."

"I'm working on that." She thought of the stuff she had in storage and asked about that. "They've gotten that too, I'm to understand. Also, the few items that were in a storage room from your mother and father. I don't know what that is, but they have it as well."

"I didn't know anything about that. I wonder what it could be?" Shrugging, they both entered the house by way of the living room. She loved this room more than any other room in the house so far. "I know it's far off, but all I've been thinking about every time I enter this room is that the holidays are going to be wonderful. I can't remember the last time that we've, grannie and Shawn, and I had enough to have a tree and a dinner. This will be epic for him."

"I'm thinking that we'll be going all out too this year. All of us are getting our families together. We have more grandchildren than I dreamed we'd have by now." She asked if she planned on spoiling them. "I do hope you're not going to be one of those mothers that gives me a list of educational things to buy for him."

"No. I think he'd have a fit if I tried that anyway. He loves things that he can work with. I've never given him a chemistry set. Frankly, I'm a tad worried about that and what he can do. But books and things like that, he loves to look at them. He's not a strong reader yet, but he's working on that too." They made their way into the kitchen and saw that all the renovations were done. And she loved it. "This is wonderful. I love that it's an eat-in kitchen as well."

After explaining about the endless refrigerator and that whatever they wanted to eat would be in it, the two of them moved to the next room and the next. Toby was making a list of things that they still needed to get, and Cindi was helping her with that too.

By the time they were ready to leave for the auction, Shawn had come home and said he wanted to go. However, after he went up to his room and saw what the faeries had done for him, he begged to stay there. Xavier was going to stay with him, and they were going to have a manly meal, whatever that meant for dinner.

"Call if you need reinforcements. Like more trucks or hands to carry things. I think that Shawn and I can fit the bill for that." Cindi drove them to the auction in the truck that had been in the driveway, and the other women were already scoping things out when they arrived. Since she'd never been to one before, she was following the advice of the people with her.

"I don't know that I feel good about spending a lot of money on some old things." They all laughed. "I'm assuming that you know something that I don't know."

"Yes. It's easy to spend more than you want to just set yourself a price and go to that. Unless you really want it, then I'd say go for it." She was wandering around just behind the others when she saw the house. It was going to be sold today as well. Toby could see her grannie living in the house. It was just like the one she'd had when Toby had been a little girl. "Get it for her if you think she'll like it. If she doesn't, the foundation will take it and use it for something. I'll help you with that."

Thanking Cindi, she thought she'd do it. But only if it didn't go for too terribly much. As soon as the auctioneer started, Toby knew that she was going to spend some money. This was wonderful.

Chapter 4

Donald wasn't sure what he was supposed to do with all this free time on his hands. His mom used to tell him that was when he did his worse planning. When he didn't have shit to occupy his mind and keep his hands busy.

Jail life wasn't for him. It never had been. Not liking to share his cell with someone was bad enough, but this system made you all eat in one common room rather than eating alone in your cell. He just hated it when people who didn't have shit to do with things decided to change things around to suit them. Like they had to justify their existence or validate their paychecks.

He wanted to have his food brought to him instead of standing in line to get whatever they flopped onto his tray. Even with all the food that they had left over, they didn't allow seconds unless you cleaned your plate completely. Like he was going to be eating shit like broccoli when there was stuff like cakes and mashed up potatoes shit that he loved. That was something else that he hated. When people didn't offer up some kind of menu when you had to be in the system. Smiling to himself, he thought that if they'd just leave him alone to do his thing, they'd not have to hear about his wants and dislikes.

"Are you going to eat that?" Ignoring the man to his left of him, Donald put his hand around his tray to show that he wasn't going to share shit. "You're a selfish prick, aren't you?"

"Fuck off." The man across from him laughed. "What the hell do you think is so funny? Do you want me to beat the shit out of you?"

"Sure, you go ahead and try that. In the meantime, you should know that there are some changes in your niece's life that will make your life a living hell if you bother her. I'm here just to inform you of what those changes are so that you don't get yourself ended by breaking my rules concerning her and that lovely little family that she had" He asked him what he was talking about. "She's under my protection. Well, under my family's protection. You might want to listen up so that you can live another day or two when you get out of here."

"Who are you talking to?" The man to his left looked confused when he pointed to the man across from him. "There ain't nobody there, dumbass. You're going to be in the hothouse if you keep this up. They don't care for crazy shit around here. Just go on and give me that bread of yours, and I'll forget that I heard you talking out of your face."

"He's sitting right there." Donald looked at the man. It only just occurred to him that he was wearing a fancy shirt and tie. Also, he was cleaned up. Like he'd done his three 'S's this morning. Shower, shit and shaved. He'd not done all three in one day since...well, it had been a fucking long time.

"No one can see or hear me but you. You might say that I'm here to warn you off your niece and your great-nephew. Also, your mother. I don't think you will do anything that I tell you, so we can just pretend like you're going to listen to me. So here it is, Donald. You come near them, and I'll kill you." He looked at the man that had told him he wasn't talking to anyone and asked him if he'd heard that. The man moved away from him to the end of the bench. Like he was nuts or something. "This is the only warning that you're going to get from me, Donald. I swear to you, if you come near what is mine, I will destroy you in ways that you can't even imagine."

The man just disappeared. Like not only had he not been there, but he couldn't smell the nice cologne that he was wearing anymore. He had only just realized. Looking around the common room, Donald wondered if he was getting like his daddy had been. Not senile, but something close to it. Talking off his noodle, his great grannie used to call it. Thinking about that now, some of the shit that his grandda used to say was funny as fuck too. Like how he was forever knowing the secret to long life. Or that he knew the combination to the bank's vault. Turned out he didn't know that last one. It got him ten years for that one.

They were lined up like kindergarteners going on a fucking field trip to go back to his room when he saw something out of the corner of his eye. As he watched the room, the dressed-up man sat down on the floor in the middle of the common room and stretched out, turning into a giant lizard. Before Donald could imagine what the hell was going on, the thing stood up on its hind legs, more than half its body in the upper floors and let out this horrible roar. It wasn't a damned lizard at all but a big fucking dragon.

When he woke up, not even realizing that he'd passed out, he was in his room on his cot. Just thinking about that monster made him shiver. Standing up and then sitting down hard, he realized that he'd been knocked about a bit. He had bumps and cuts all over his arms and neck. They'd must have beaten him a little to get him in here without his screaming. And he knew that he had. The dragon had put his face right up close to him. At least he remembered that part.

Eyeing the urinal on the wall and then looking down at himself, he wasn't sure that he wanted to try taking a piss again, either. The last time he'd tried, it had been like he'd bitten down into a juicy lemon, rind and all and that was how his pecker had felt. The bitterness and the pain of it had made tears roll down his face. Blood, too, had come out of him. Not a lot of it then, but he knew that if he were to go try and take a piss now, he'd spring a leak so bad that they'd find him all drained out at bed check time. His bladder was backing up so much right now he was sure that he was eyeing things with a yellow hue around them.

Standing up, staggering to the wall, Donald held onto the concrete brick with one hand and his dick with the other. Being as careful as he could, not wanting to squeeze his manly part too much, he closed his eyes and begged his peter to just let it be not too painful.

The first little drop off the end of his dick didn't even phase him. So trying just for a bit more, Donald turned his face into his arm, holding onto the wall and bit down on his flesh so he'd not scream out in pain. As soon as his teeth sank into his arm, he knew that he'd just made the biggest mistake of his life in using his own body to stop the pain.

Blood filled his mouth, and sweat, too, poured off his face in rivers. Even as he sobbed, begging for his dick to just come off and be done with it, he bit himself harder. The pain was endless. His body, stiff with it, seemed to have a mind of its own in that it wanted to punish him for something and let go of a stream of blood so thick that he was surely going to lose the biggest part of his dick. Still trying his best not to squeeze his dick right off his body, he had to stand there, crying with his dick in his hand and his mouth on his arm, when someone behind him asked him if he was all right.

When commanded to turn around, he had to. Donald had been in prison or jail setting for more than half his life. Without looking at the man to gauge his reaction to what he was seeing, Donald went to his knees and then fell face forward onto the floor. The last thing he felt was his head bouncing off the concrete twice before he wasn't in any more pain.

~*~

"I can honestly say that I don't think I've seen an infection like Donald's in all my life of being a jail surgeon. And those kidney stones that he was trying to pass were as big as a pea. We took out three of them suckers after we were able to bust them up into smaller stones. I don't envy him when he wakes up.

Small wonder he'd been able to urinate at all before today." Dover tried very hard not to laugh. It wasn't the story that was being told about Donald that had him laughing but the doctor who had been telling him about it. Doctor Kelly simply told it like it was, and be damned how it might sound to others. "Finding him there on the floor like I did, it sure did do my heart some good, I tell you, son. The way he'd been treating others all these years, it was nice to see him getting his comeuppance. But him lying there with his dick in one hand and his arm all bloodied on the other side of him was worth every penny of my med school years. Every durn penny of it."

"Will he be all right?" Grannie, Toby's grandmother, had asked him to call her looked like she was enjoying the story as well. "Damned old fool. I told him when he was little that he needed to take care of that body of his. That he wasn't going to be getting a do-over when he fucked up. Even taught the little shit how to go about cleaning that part of him so that he'd not get any infections that even penicillin wouldn't take care of. Did he listen? No. He's as big a fool as his brother. Daniel is as dumb as a rock, but I'm betting that he'd know better than to let one of them rocks go through where only his piss is supposed to go. What did you have to do to his arm? I'm assuming that you had to sew that flap he made back in place."

"Had to get him relaxed enough to get it out of his mouth first. He bit himself so hard that I was sure that he'd bitten into bone and whatnot." They all laughed then when Doc Kelly acted out getting Donald's teeth unclenched. "It was like fighting a gator, I tell you. But once we got him loosened up, it was easy sailing then. Poor idiot. He isn't going to be in a good mood when he wakes up, I betcha."

Dover made his way home from the hospital. He had plenty of things to do today, and hanging around the hospital wasn't getting anything done. He had to get his ass in gear before he saw his dad again. He'd been the one that had given him the list last night. Even Toby had a list of things she was doing. However, she'd made up her own list.

"I don't know what this means." He glanced over at the paperwork that was in front of his brother, Hedley. They'd been sharing an office since they'd moved here. "I mean, I know what it means. I just don't know what it's supposed to mean for the foundation. It's telling me that there are several donations that haven't been accepted by the charity that was set up for them, like this first one here. It says that the money that is earmarked is for non-perishable food. The other one is for the storage of the food. Why aren't they doing what they asked for in the way of the money coming in?"

"So we've put money aside for the storage of the food, right?" Hedley nodded and showed him the receipt of the two storage cabinets being delivered to the place. "I'd make a call to see if they're waiting on someone to come in and build the units."

"They're put together as of the day that they were delivered. There are locks, too, to put on the units that are still in the packaging, according to Cloe, the faerie that I sent to check on it. Also, and this one boggles my mind, there is a list hanging on the doors of the two units as to what is supposed to be going into them. Yet nothing has been purchased." Dover asked him what the last donation was for. "Refrigeration. Two large freezers and a large refrigerator that will hold things that they use daily. Milk, eggs, things like that. They've been sitting in the box they were delivered in for three weeks now. As far as I can tell, they're ordering pizzas and subs for the people there instead of cooking as they had wanted."

"Well, I think that the two of us need to talk to someone about this. I have time now if you do." Hedley said that he had more than enough time to get this fixed up as they were now asking for more money to feed the people. "I guess I should have asked this first, but what kind of place is this? I'm assuming that it's some sort of shelter or something."

"It's the women's prison release program building. The building has been in use for two weeks now, and I thought it seemed to be doing just fine. Some of the women there are cooking their own food with a voucher that we set up for them to purchase food in town. But for the most part, they were supposed to be fed at least one meal a day. The vouchers aren't made to feed someone three meals a day." He asked if they could add more to the voucher. "I've looked into this, and that is how I figured out that the cafeteria isn't being used as we wanted. The dining area is full of storage, like the units and extra things like beds and such. The kitchen is just this hollow place where the appliances are, but nothing is being used. There is also a semi on the lot that is holding the non-perishable things until the shelves, and other units are set up. It's like tumble down shit. Nothing is started so that the things can flow into one another."

"All right. We'll have a look around then we'll decide what needs to be done. Like you said, it might just be a simple thing like no one has clue one on how to put the things together." Dover called out for Cleo since she had the most contact with the building. Asking her to gather up some more faeries to help with the place, she looked so relieved that he wondered why she'd not said anything to Hedley. "I'm not sure what is needed, but I'm sure that you can get on it right away if necessary."

"We can do anything you wish, sir." When she left them, he looked at Hedley. It had come to his attention that his brother seemed to be in over his head about things. Asking him about it seemed to be the most straightforward way of getting to the bottom of it.

"I don't know what's wrong with me. I find

myself drifting in and out of thoughts with no rhyme nor reason all the time lately. Like this morning. I was eating a bowl of cereal and watching the news when I realized that it was noon. I haven't any idea what I did in those five hours between getting me something to eat and the noon news coming on." He asked if he'd talked to anyone else about it. "No. I wouldn't even know how to start that conversation. 'By the way, I'm losing my mind. Can you tell me if that's normal or not?' Not that I think I'm losing my mind, but things just aren't flowing as I want them to. Not even having a list to follow is helping me."

"If I were you, I'd talk to mom or dad. Maybe it's something they know about. I don't think that you're losing your mind either, but you're not well if you ask me." He said that he felt well but not all there. "That's even scarier, Hedley. Talk to them soon too. It might just be a simple matter of you taking on too much right now, and you're overwhelmed."

They were pulling into the lot when Cleo joined them. She said that they could start in the kitchen area right now and put it to rights. Without knowing what was going on, he asked her to wait. As he and his brother had been talking about, it might just be a simple matter of just getting started.

The kitchen was just as he'd been told. Nothing was in place, and while it looked like it had been cleaned up when it had been put in, now it was dusty and cluttered with items that hadn't been used yet. Setting the faeries to work, he entered what was supposed to be the dining area. He was surprised to see a lone woman putting tables together.

"Do you need help?" She stared at him for a second, then nodded. "I thought that this was all done, or we would have come out sooner. I'm sorry for the delay."

"I asked that woman that is in charge of the kitchen if she was going to start cooking meals in here, and she said that she didn't have the authority to do that. Why the hell would you hire a cook that isn't allowed to cook when people are hungry." He told her that he'd not been aware of anything like that. "Yeah, I didn't think so. I love staying here, don't get me wrong. But I think we were treated better in prison. At least someone cooked us a decent meal daily."

"I'm taking care of the kitchen as we speak. Also,

we'll get this place put together now. I'm assuming that you're aware that we're not human." She said she didn't care if he was a dragon so long as they had a meal to sit down to. "Funny you should say that. I and my brother both are dragons. We're having faeries work on the kitchen now, and it should be finished soon. Also, as soon as you're willing to step back, they'll have this set to right in less time than we could do it."

"Go for it then. I don't cook. I'm sick to death of eating noodles that are harder than my head for each meal. And if I never see another peanut butter sandwich again, I'll be a happy person." Cleo came into the room and set to work. "They are fast."

For the most part, it was a blur of activity while the room was put to rights. Not only did they get things put together, but the food was brought in and set up in the units as well. Within an hour, not only was the room finished, but it resembled a nice restaurant with plants on the tables as well as tablecloths.

It was only at the end that other women showed up to help out. Once they were all assembled, the woman, her name was Jane Hopkins, started organizing the women into groups to start cooking. He loved her skills at delegating work and also how she didn't just hand out assignments, but she also had herself a list of things that she was going to do.

By the time they left the place, he had a feeling that there would be no more trouble at the place. The cook, the one that they'd hired to do the kitchen work, was fired on the spot when Hedley noticed that she was on drugs. She made a big stink about how it was our fault that she'd been doing them because we'd not been checking up on her daily so that she could do better.

Whatever. As they were leaving the place, he was ready to go home and work on some projects. Talking to Hedley again about his fog, he decided to drop him off at their parent's home so that he could get a start on whatever was going on. He knew that if mom or dad didn't know what was wrong, they'd find someone that could tell them.

Toby was at the house when he got there. She had gotten a shipment of things that she was going to use at the shelter to help with computer skills, as well as teaching some of them to read and write. He knew what she might be going through with this, it was difficult enough teaching children, but an adult had to be much harder. He asked her about it.

"It isn't, actually. They've lived without the simple knowledge that most of us take for granted for a long time. They have to second guess everything they do, from buying groceries to just being able to order from a menu. These women want to learn so that they're not feeling left behind." He said he'd not thought of that. "There is one woman. Her name is Betsy. She told me that she was the high school prom queen. Was the president of her class and on her way to college when she realized that she didn't have the first clue as to how to read the applications to get into one. It was her parent's fault, she told me. They got her what she wanted by her good looks. I told her that she had a brain and she should have used it instead of being prom queen. Because that wasn't going to pay the bills. I thought for sure she was going to be pissy with me, but she didn't. I think she's going to do well now that she realizes what she's been missing."

"How could a person go through school without knowing the basics of reading? I mean, really? How would you even get to your classes and such?" Toby told him that she'd floated along with the crowd and was able to hide it that way. "That is the saddest thing I've ever heard, I think. I'm assuming that she can at least read a little, right?"

"She knows her alphabet well. Can sound out words when she gets to one that she doesn't know. And if that doesn't work, she just skips it and tries to get what the meaning is from the rest of the words. Usually, she said that it would work for her. But as she got older and the words got harder, plus she told me she just got lazier, it was difficult for her to fudge her way through." He asked her why she was in prison. "She murdered her boyfriend when he found out that she wasn't able to read the menu one night. He humiliated her right there, and she took a glass, broke it off on the table and cut his throat."

"That seems sort of extreme." Toby told him what had really happened. "So it was bottled up inside of her all that time, and when he outed her in public, it seemed to make her snap? I guess I can see that too. But damn, she ruined her life by killing some jerk."

"She did. And had to go to prison. But that is where she found herself lacking in her life. Betsy said that had she not killed him, then she would have more than likely killed her parents or, worse, a bunch of people. It got her to deal with things in a better setting than she was doing for herself. The boyfriend was an asshole, as it turned out that he'd been cruel to a lot of people in high school. All women that were having trouble with one thing or another — mostly self-esteem issues and mental breakdowns. Also, she found out that he wasn't nearly as smart as he projected himself to be. He was a football jock and skated along on that when he was in high school and on into college."

"Still seems like a bad reason to kill someone. But then, I've not had that sort of issues growing up. I didn't have a lot of trouble with my self-esteem, nor did I have anyone around that would make fun of me unless it was just that, a joke." Toby told him that he was very lucky. "I'm beginning to see that. There are a lot of people, not just women, that could use a dose of good vibes coming their way."

"You're right. There are a great many kids that need it, too, like the kids in this family. Most of them have grown up to be self-aware about their surroundings but not what to do about them when cornered. I think, and this is just me, that all the family needs to help with their life experiences with the kids so that they're better prepared for living forever. I know that I could use a little help with that." He said that pacing yourself is what needs to be done. "You learned that from your parents. What about the kids that had no parents before coming here? My son being one of them."

They hadn't talked about Shawn all the much about his being magical. He still hadn't been to see his grandfather, which, until Andar was ready to sit down and talk to them, wasn't going to happen. Winnie had been called in twice now to talk to Andar, and so far, from what he heard, the man was coming to reason. Whatever that meant for Shawn and Toby.

"Shawn is at your parent's house tonight. Your dad has some projects that he wants to get some input from him about. I'm not sure what that could be, but Cindi said she'd keep an eye on the two of them so that they'd not get into too much trouble. Does that happen often?" Dover laughed and said, with his dad, it was always happening. "That's sort of what your mom said. Xavier likes to stir up trouble when he can with his brothers."

"He does. Being the youngest of them, dad has always been a bit on the trouble side. Not that he was ever cruel or mean, but he'd start talking about things until it was all around the family that so and so was doing something insane. Like one time, he let on that Lincoln was dating an older woman. Like a very older woman. Turned out that dad just wanted to embarrass his brother. It worked, but he also got the shit knocked out of him." Toby asked if he'd learned anything from it. "Yes. To hear dad talk about it, all he learned was to run faster when Lincoln was after him. It's all in good fun. But when they're needed as a whole, I've never seen anyone come together like they do."

"I've noticed that about all of you. When there is a need, you guys will form a circle around each other that nothing can penetrate." He said that was what saved them more than one time in their life. "I can imagine. Before I forget. The eggs are starting to deplete faster than they're coming in. I don't know why that's important, but I was told to let you know."

"It means that all the eggs are being taken care of." She nodded and stared at him for a few seconds before he smiled at her. "What's bothering you? Certainly, not the egg situation, is it?"

"No. I'm just very proud of the fact that you guys saw a need for the eggs and did something about it. I'm sure there will be a great many dragons out there that will have children when they didn't think they ever would. Imp certainly is happy that they're going to be hatched soon too." He said that they were as well. "I've never seen a baby dragon. I imagine that they look just like you do, only smaller."

"Yes. Well, it would depend on the dragon, I guess. I'm a pearl dragon, so I can blend into anything that is around me. When I was small, mom was forever having to find me because of it. I didn't know what I was doing back then. Mom finally had to put a bell around my neck so that she could locate me when it was necessary for me to come into the house. As for looking like a smaller version of my adult self, I think my mom has a book of pictures around here that could answer that question. Raising a dragon nowadays would be so much easier, I was told. There are any number of places where they can be hidden and not bothered. Being able to become human when necessary has saved every one of us in some way. My grandparents weren't able to shift. But he gave up his life to make it so that his sons and their children would be safer than he was. I can't love them anymore for that."

"I wish I could have known them. I wish that I could have known all of the dragons before you guys." He said that Imp could show her whatever she wanted to see. "She's special, isn't she? I mean, to have been able to think of such magnificent creatures and make them a reality. It's more than I think that anyone could have done to brighten the world around them."

"You should tell her that. She loves her dragons and would love to hear that you love them as much as she does." Toby said she'd do that. "Good. All right. How about we go get some dinner out and then go by my parent's house to see the books."

"Better idea. Let's invite your parents to go with us, and we'll talk about it over dinner. Sometimes I like them more than you." They were still laughing when they headed upstairs to change. Dover couldn't believe his luck in finding a mate. He thought about his brother and wondered if that was all he needed. A mate to settle his mind and help him out. Time would tell, he supposed. He wanted his little brother as happy as he was. As happy as all of them were.

Chapter 5

Toby decided to walk home from the shelter. It was a beautiful afternoon, and she was going to enjoy the weather as much as she could. As she was going past one of the shops that were forever popping up around town nowadays, she noticed that Shawn was in one of them. While she didn't want to check up on him, she did go in and acted surprised to see him there. She asked him what he was doing.

He was surprised to see her. "Checking things out. I thought about what Dover told me about doing some good around town. You know, looking into things so that I can see if there is anything that I can do to make things easier. Not just on the people shopping but the store itself." She told him that was a good thing to do. "Yeah. So far, I'm not sure what I'm doing."

Toby was proud of his initiative. "What you're doing right now is a start. Just looking around, observing things. That's how this works." He nodded but didn't look all that convinced that he was doing anything productive. "Look around. What do you see right now? I don't mean the shop items, but what would you do, as a little boy, to make shopping here easier for someone as tall as you are. And so you know, you're also going to be helping elderly people with your thoughts that aren't able to do much either. For one reason or another, they might well be in a wheelchair or just simply too banged up to do what you can do easily."

He looked around. She could tell that he was bothered by the things on the upper shelves. She would be too, she supposed, if she were a child that wanted to have a look at the toys stored up there. It was a shame, really, she thought that they weren't down where kids with a few bucks could purchase them. But this was his project, and she'd not tell him what to see in the room.

"They have a lot of boxes on the top shelves of things that I'd like to look at. Like those bobblehead things. But when I asked if I could have a ladder, they told me that I'm not allowed to step up on one." She told him it was more than likely an insurance thing. "Yeah, that's what she told me. But it's hard to look at them when they have them up so high. Do you suppose they don't want to sell them?"

"I doubt that they'd invest in something with no plans of selling them." She looked at the place where Shawn was talking about. "They are terribly high, aren't they. I wonder if they have some way of bringing them down to them when someone wants to purchase them. I don't know. Like one of those pinchy things that you can pick things up from the floor." He pointed to the counter, and she saw a couple of them hanging behind them on the wall. "Okay, so we've figured that out. What would you do to improve your being able to look before you buy things like that?"

"I don't know. I guess I can understand why they'd put them up high. I mean, I'd like them, but they seem to sell a lot of other stuff in here, okay." She watched as he looked around. "Really, mom, I think it's just too crowded in here. Like they're using every space available to them to stuff the store. It's hard to figure out if you want anything because there is just too much to choose from. Don't you think?"

She agreed with him. Toby also told him that she'd not seen that. But it was very crowded to even walk around the things at their level. She asked him what he'd do about it. If it were his shop.

"Go to a bigger place. Or maybe just expand out or something. Not to put more things in the shop but to get things down to a level where people like me can see what they want. I might even get rid of a lot of this stuff that has dust on it. I don't think that looks good when it's dusty. It looks like nobody cares about it." He grinned at her and shrugged his shoulders. "But what do I know? I'm just a kid."

Laughing, Toby thought that his ideas were wonderful. Especially the part where he was thinking of not putting more products in but to bring things to a certain height so that everyone could shop in comfort.

They made their way to the next couple of shops. She was glad for this time for the two of them. Lately, with all the new things going on in their life, they'd not had a great deal of just the two of them time. Dover met them at the last shop they were in. Toby encouraged Shawn to tell Dover what they'd been doing.

"Excellent. So you know, the shop that you said needs to expand had been approached by the foundation to see if they'd like to do that. He said he was making a living and that he didn't want to change things up at his age. I think he's had enough of shop ownership, and when he sells out, the foundation will more than likely buy him out and do just as you suggested. Good call, Shawn. I'm proud of you."

The two of them were getting along well, she realized. It was good for Shawn to have a male in his life — not that Dover was the only male figure in his life all of a sudden with all his brothers — but they were also enjoying each other's company too. They never let her feel left out, either. Having her join in their plotting, what she often thought they were doing when their heads were together.

"How about I take my two favorite people out to dinner tonight, and tomorrow we work on getting the house in order. My parents have set aside some of the things that they thought that we could incorporate into the house." Shawn asked him about the sword collection that he'd told him about. "Yes, my dad said that if you come over sometime, he'll show them all to you. Dad is excited to have someone fresh hear his stories, so be prepared to hear them a great deal over the next few decades."

Dinner was nice. Dover told them about his brother and how his mom had said it was stress that was putting him in a fog. She suggested that he rest more during the day and let his mind settle about things when he gets overwhelmed. Toby thought that was a good idea for everyone. Cindi was making him take a week or two off to go to an island that Winnie owned to not be able to talk to anyone over the phone or computer. Toby had heard about the island and thought that it might be a good place for a honeymoon someday.

"I bet he'll hate that a lot." Dover laughed with Shawn. "I've never had a cell phone until coming here. But I don't use it as much as some kids I know. It's nice to look things up on, but I don't have anyone to call. That mind thing really helps when I have a question about something. Even grannie likes that she can just talk to me when she wants to."

"I do that too. Talk to my mom when I have a question or just to tell her that I love her. And it works out really well when you're in a crowded room, and you don't remember someone's name. I've used that a lot over the last couple of months. Mom and dad seem to know everyone." She enjoyed using the mind thing for those reasons and more. Like when she was afraid or upset, she knew that Dover could—

She loved him. It hit her hard in the face that she was actually in love with Dover and not having a clue how that happened. Well, she did have a clue. He was the kindest, most perfect man she'd ever met. And he was good to her grannie and son. The two of them turned to look back at her as they were walking home, and Dover asked her if she was all right.

"I love you." He grinned like a kid who had gotten everything that he wanted for Christmas and more. "I know I should have worked up to it, just blurting it out like I did. But it just hit me. I'm in love with you."

"I've loved you since the moment that I saw you." He kissed her then, much to the embarrassment to Shawn. "It's a wonderful feeling, isn't it? To be loved and to be in love. I don't think that I ever thought that I'd have someone to —"

Suddenly they were surrounded by tiny creatures. They didn't look like faeries. She knew that they weren't when Andar was standing in front of her and Dover. Something was wrong. It took her a moment to realize that they were surrounded and that the arrows that were at the ready were pointed outward and not toward them. Also, Andar was bleeding.

"There are several men nearby that are planning to take one or both of you, Toby. If you would allow it, I'll make sure that you're safe until the threat is taken care of." She asked him if he was all right. The shock on his face was a surprise. "I don't believe anyone has asked that of me since…well, I don't believe that they have ever asked. I am well. Only a small wound that I got when rushing from my home to here."

"Do you know what they want from us?" He glanced at Dover and then back at her. "You don't have to run things through him, Andar. If you know the answer, then you should just tell me before I have to beat the shit out of you for holding back. I'm afraid and nervous. Spill it, or I'll beat it out of you."

He threw back his head and laughed. "One moment, you're making sure I am all right. The next willing to do bodily harm to me should I not do as you wish. They only wish to gain control over a piece of jade. At first, I thought it odd. What would a person want to kidnap over a thing that is in abundance in my world. But I remember hearing about a certain teapot." Dover said that his uncle had it. "Yes, I had heard that as well. The jade piece, it has great value because of the magic that it took to carve it. I am envious of not being able to see such a piece, but they had hoped to take you and then have whoever owns it; they don't know who, at this point, will gladly turn it over to them. But alas, I do believe that they'd kill your—or try to kill you when they were finished."

"I need to get with my family on this. Toby had come here to warn us about the piece. But to be honest, I've not thought of it since." He stepped away to no doubt talk to his brothers. But he turned at the last moment to smile and put out his hand for the king. "Andar, I'm grateful for you watching over my family. I will have to give you a gift for such fast thinking."

She noticed that he'd not said that he didn't owe him anything. "You are confused. Is it about the gift? To turn one down is considered a terrible breach of protocol. Especially when the giver is the nephew of the king of all dragons. Even if he only gives me a chance to look at the jade, it would be more than anything that I could imagine as a gift from him."

"Are we still in danger?" He shook his head and smiled. "But the fae, they're still here. Aren't you afraid that someone will see them? Especially dressed the way that they are? The armor is beautiful, but I'm sure that they have better things to do than to stand around like this."

"I wish for others to see them. Some do, but most do not, which is all right as well. If word gets around that you're fully protected at all times, perhaps someone will think twice about coming for you." She asked him if that worked. "Most of the time, it does. But it's the determined ones that it doesn't. For they think that they are justified in their actions and are quite surprised when things do not turn out the way they think or hope they should. As for this army, they are around you and Shawn at all times. They are seen today, as you pointed out, to make sure that it is known that you're under my protection as well as the dragons."

She looked at the men and women around her. "They'd die for us, wouldn't they?" Andar only nodded. "I can't thank you enough for your help in this and other things I'm sure that you're doing behind my back. I don't like it, but I do appreciate it immensely. Thank you."

When she put her hand on the shoulder of the fae warrior next to her to thank him as well, she felt a wave of despair that frightened her a little. Turning the man around so that she could see his face, she wasn't surprised to see that he was sporting not just a black eye but a busted lip as well. However, she didn't think that everyone could see his wounds. But somehow, by touching him, she was privy to them.

"Your boss did this." He answered even though it wasn't a question that she was indeed correct. *"Are there others like you? Ones that he takes to task when he is in trouble at his home?"*

"Many, my lady. I'm only a cog in his wheel, he tells me. Also, should I talk to anyone about his treatment, it will

be harder on my family." She didn't bother telling him that she was going to be a cog in his wheel very soon. *"My lady?"*

"You're going to be all right. And I thank you for not lying to me." He said that he couldn't even if he wanted to. *"Then I doubly thank you for that. But this isn't going to be happening to anyone anymore. If he is having trouble at work, there is no reason for him to take it out on the people that work for him. Not today."* She looked at Andar. "You said that I was your right-hand man, so to speak."

"You are. And just so you're aware of it, I had no idea that you'd be able to communicate with the men surrounding you. It's a good thing, don't get me wrong, but I'm sorry that I didn't think of it soon. What would you need from me, my lady?" She told him that she wanted to see the man in charge of such people that would lay down their lives for her. "That can be arranged. I only have about a hundred fae helping with this task. I could and would add more should you need it. But this is a good thing that you wish to congratulate him on a job well done."

"Yes, well, we'll see about that." Andar looked confused but didn't ask. Suddenly she was in a chamber room that was as beautifully, over-the-top done as she'd ever seen. There was tea, a thing that she was beginning to get used to drinking all the time and some fruit. Toby much preferred it over the sweet scones, but when she was angry, as she was now, she would eat just about anything. The man was brought forth to her almost as soon as they were all seated. She looked at the man and knew something about him that she was sure that his own wife didn't.

"You beat your men and women so that you can get a sexual thrill out of it. You will step down as leader to these men, return their monies and restore the families that you have torn apart with your overstepping your bounds." The man, Denny, looked at her and at Andar. "I'm in charge at the moment. Did you really think that you could just go about beating and killing people simply because you frightened them so badly that they'd do what you said?"

"I didn't...I don't know what you're talking about, my lady." She only had to stand up, and then so did her son and Andar. Neither of them stepped in front of her, which made her feel empowered. "I wish you no harm, my lady, but I don't know where this is coming from. I'm a good leader. These men are loyal to me, and I to them. I might knock them about a bit to show them…what is the meaning of this, my lord? You bring me here to have this female accuse me of something that is untrue? I don't know what to think about any of this."

"So I'm to understand. But only when you get your way. The cogs, as you have called them on more than one occasion, will be free of you as of this very moment." Again, Denny looked at Andar. She just knew he wasn't going to back her up on this, and she really was going to hurt the old king. "You've been beating them, kidnapping their children only to sell them off to the highest bidder, then, if that wasn't enough, you'd rape their wives while they were chained to the wall."

"My lady, surely you jest." She only cocked a brow at Denny, and he seemed to crumble under the weight of her stare. "You're not going to come in here and accuse me of anything without proof. And there is no one, not a single person that is beneath me that will open their mouths to say any differently."

"Won't they." With a snap of her fingers—truly she had no idea where this knowledge was coming from that she was using came from, all the men in the room, including some of the children that were feeding the goats, looked like they did to her when she'd first appeared. "This is your handy work. All of it. And the worse part is, you've been doing it for centuries, and no one has ever taken you to task over it." Denny laughed. Asking her why anyone would care about his methods after all this time. "I do, and that is why I'm going to make sure you're stopped."

Denny disappeared. There wasn't a sound for several long moments until she looked at Andar. "Where did he go?" She looked at Andar as if he'd done it then it hit her. "It was me. I must have dealt with him, but I didn't realize I could." She was dumbfounded. "You knew…." Taking a step back from the man, his anger weighed heavily on his features.

Shawn took her hand. "He was a bad man, mom. You stopped him."

Andar shook himself before he spoke. "No, I didn't know." She nodded, but she was still puzzled on how she'd simply made the man disappear. "No. I should have known. I should have been aware of things that…how much more have you figured out in being here only a quarter of an hour?"

When Toby sat back down in her chair, they all sat. "I don't know what is considered going on, but a great many things are wrong here." When Andar didn't object, she continued. "I wouldn't take all the blame, but a big part of it is your lack of seeing to things that you should be. However, just to name a few, your jade is being sold on the black market through the internet. I don't know yet who is taking it. Also, your kitchen staff needs to be terminated if you're not going to be using them. They're feeding their own families with the riches that you have brought here in the event you wish for something. I do believe that some of your staff own a few more pieces of land that you once owned. If you want a steak, go someplace on the other side to have it. I'm surprised they haven't tried to poison you as yet." Toby was surprised when Andar laughed. He seemed to be getting used to it. The sound and the way it made him feel. It even tugged at her own lips to join him. "You believe me."

Andar nodded and looked very pleased with himself. "I do. It's not because you're a woman but because you have fresh eyes when you came here. As for why it's coming to you, I'd say that it had been coming to me too, but I, unlike you, have ignored it for other things. Things that, while wrong, I deemed unimportant to me." She nodded and was happy to see she was getting through to him. "All right. Let's work together on this jade business. While there is a great deal of it around here, to flood the market with it from here would make it valueless to those that actually do find it and sell it for a good profit."

She worked with him for over three hours. Not only did the staff get fired, but he also figured out that the jades were being stolen and resold by the gardeners. It wasn't anything for them to get permission from the faerie queen to get some faeries to his place to clean up the castle too.

~*~

Donald didn't have any idea where he was for several minutes. It smelled clean, which is what threw him off. His prison cell never smelled that good. And there was very little sound. When he was able to keep his eyes open for more than a few seconds, he realized then that he was in a hospital. Not only that but he was chained to the bed with both arms and ankles. He saw the little nurse before she realized that he was awake. Startling her was fun for him until his laughter nearly caused him to pass out again.

"Yeah, I'd watch any kind of sudden movement for a while. They had to operate on your groin area to remove the kidney stones that were lodged in your penis. You're lucky that you didn't get more damage done to yourself, Donald." He asked her what she was talking about. "Surgery. You know what that means, I'm assuming." Donald nodded, still not sure what she was talking about. "Well, they had to go along your urethra and break up the larger stones that had gotten in there and were causing you to be unable to urinate. Once they were able to clear a pathway out, the infection set in, and you've been on a catheter for the last few days to keep you still and get the poison out of your system."

"I've had them before. They just give me some drugs until it passes then I'm all right. Why did they have to—are you saying that they operated on my dick?" She smiled at him, and he noticed that she was never close enough for him to cuff a time a two too. He wanted to do that more than anything when she laughed all the time. "What did they do to my dick? If they cut it open, there is going to be hell to pay."

"I think they opted for just breaking up the stones that were lodged in there rather than trying to find a way to cut into that tiny member you have." He told her to come over here, and she'd show him not tiny his dick was. For some reason, that didn't sound right. When she laughed, Donald saw red. However, the pain in his dick was terrible when he reached out to grab the woman. "You're as stupid as they come, aren't you? So you know, I'm not tempted to see what you have or do not have in your member." He jerked on the cuffs again, and the pain spasmed. Before he could ask her what sort of membership she was talking about, a man came into the room with them.

"Hello, Donald. You know, if you don't start taking care of yourself, you're going to end up on the wrong side of a coffin." He said he was doing just fine, then told him what the woman had said to him. "Woman? You mean your niece? Christ man, don't you even know your relatives when you see them? Perhaps Toby was right. You did lose a great many brain cells when they took out the stones in your body."

Toby laughed at the shocked look on Donald's face and answered the man. "We never got around to it. You'd think because he'd seen me just the other day, he'd have a clue, but I'm thinking that he's just stupid." Donald yanked on the cuffs again and grunted in pain as they continued to ignore him. "Did you get Shawn off to Andar already?" The man said that they'd had a nice lunch and were going to work on the magic that was Shawn's. "Oh, good. I'm glad that we're not at each other's throats all the time. Makes it easier for me to—"

"What the good fuck are you talking about?" They both looked at him as if they'd forgotten he was in the room with them. "I want you to bail me out of here, Toby. You and I have some shit that needs to be taken care of. And where is my mom? She should be here making sure that I have all that I need."

Toby crossed her arms over her chest defiantly. "You have all that you're going to get. You're going to prison as soon as you leave here." He asked her why. "Why? I thought you'd have a long list of shit that should put you in prison by now. But mostly, it's because when the police were sent to your home, they found the bank bags from three recent robberies."

"I don't know what you're talking about." Toby rolled her eyes at him. "You'll get me out of here, Toby, or so help me, I'm going to make you regret being my niece."

Toby snorted. "Well, that's already a reality. I hate being related to you." He didn't understand why she'd say something like that to him. He was her fucking uncle. "You are, but since you're nothing but a pain in the ass, I'm going to wash my hands of you and not have a thing to do with you after this."

"Shelby. What does he think about that?" She asked him who that was. "Your fucking son, you moron. And they think that I should be locked up. He's your kid, dumbass. And my favorite nephew."

Toby rolled her eyes again. "His name is Shawn, not Shelby. And he's your only nephew. Not that it makes any difference to him, but he's not going to be coming around you, either. You're going to be put away so that you and my dad can live out your lives without being able to cause too much in the way of trouble." She stared at him and then laughed. "Though it's doubtful that you'll try and behave, but like I said,

I don't care."

"You will care when I get out of here, Toby. I'm sick of you acting like your shit don't stink. You will do as you're told and be quick about it." They left him there by going out the door without even a 'see you soon.' "You get your ass back here, Toby Deaver. I swear to you, I should have hit you more as a kid."

His dick was hurting him now. When he pulled the blanket off his legs to have a look at what they'd done to him. What he saw was this long assed tube sticking in the end of it with blood and yellow piss in it. Sick to his belly, thinking how painful it was to have that thing sticking out of his dick, he laid his head back and counted to ten. About all he could count to and not mess up too badly.

Punching the call light several times to get some help, he found himself snarling at Toby and her man as to how this was their fault that he was hurting. Whoever the fuck he was to her anyway. He screamed at them about how they should go out on the streets and get him the good stuff. Not that they heard him, but he was on a roll now. The nurse, a big burly looking man, told him to behave or he might just call the police to hold him down while he gave him the drugs.

"Just fucking do your job. I'm hurting, and I'll sue your ass if you don't get that shit in me right now. And don't think I'm going to be given that watered-down shit, either. I want a full-on hardon when that shit is put in my system." The nurse just laughed at him. When he turned on his heel and left him, Donald leapt towards the nurse and pulled on the tube in his dick and fell out of the fucking bed. Because he was still cuffed, the bed and all came crashing to the floor on top of him. The last thing he felt was his dick. He was sure it was being ripped from his body.

Chapter 6

Dover enjoyed his time at the house with his family. Mom and dad were supposed to come over later, so now it was just he, Toby and Shawn. Toby was learning to use her wings, and Shawn, while he had them as well, seemed to be getting used to them better than his mom. However, he didn't make fun of or tease his mom but helped her when she asked. Toby landed, for only about the third time, on her feet after lifting herself from the grass.

"You should take your shoes off." Dover thought that this idea had merit, too but watched mother and son talking about it. "You could get some help from the earth. Anything really but the dirt is yours to use too."

"Are you saying that I need to get my feet dirty to fly like you?" He grinned at her and told his mom that he'd never do that. "I should hope not. You're hard enough to keep clean after being out in the yard all day. Is this why you wanted to come out in the back yard to do this?"

"No. I like the outdoors. I think that it has a lot to do with what I am, but I do love being outside." She ruffled his hair and told him she loved him. "I love you too, mom. You're a good mom, and I think that I have the best of the best with you."

"I love you too, son." They worked for another hour on landing, just until his parents arrived. "We were practicing."

"Practicing things like landing isn't nearly as important as taking off. You want to be comfortable with being able to get out of a situation more than you do, landing to be in the middle of things again." Dad talked about when he was younger, how there had been times, as a pearl dragon himself, that he had to take off and become something in the woods behind where they were staying."

"I never thought of that. I just thought that landing not on my head would keep me safe." Dad told her how she was never going to be able to use her magic in an emergency situation if she wasn't comfortable with it in the first place. "All right. I'm assuming that you might have an idea how I can get this better?"

"No. None at all. I don't know the point where you might want to flee rather than fight. That's up to you. However, don't discount the fact that you have shields around you at all times. Magic out the ass and that you're immortal. Usually, now more than ever, I stick around to try and fix whatever is going on. I'm much too old to be taking off at a second's notice when I can watch something that I might find funny in a couple of days." Dad wasn't all that serious about what he was saying to Toby, but she took it as such. When she asked him in what way would she need to get away from something. "If there is a fire or something, and you need to get Shawn away quickly."

"Even a house fire where there are mortal people living." Dad then told her that he'd been kidding her and that she could do whatever she wanted. "No, perhaps you were, but this makes me see what I need to do. If I'm so wrapped up in landing on my feet and not my ass, I might hesitate in doing the right thing. Thanks, Xavier."

Dad came and sat down next to him. "Your mate is very literal, isn't she? Cindi told me the other day that she was surprised at how much she didn't know about her magic, and it was like she had to beat it into her head that sex is what gave it to her." Dad laughed. "Well, it wasn't that bad, but it was shocking to Toby to know that was how she'd been able to have any."

"She told me about it. Also, how mom had been so helpful to her about other things too. I don't know why she thought this, but Toby thought that the other women wouldn't want to include her in things as she's not been here as long as they have. I thought she was joking, but apparently, she wasn't." Dad said that his mom was the last to come to the family with his brothers. "Yes, I told Toby that too, and she was happy that they'd 'made an effort' for my mom. That's when I realized that she's not met the rest of the family. Do you suppose they'll want to get together soon to meet her as well? I can hold them off until Headley finds his mate if you think that'll help."

"I would say that it would be easier for you to just tell them to come instead of trying to coordinate something where we can all be together. In fact, that's what I would suggest you do, stay out of it. I'm sure that by now, they're setting up plans to come here without anyone being the wiser." He said that more than likely, they'd done all the background checks and were completely satisfied with her. "You can bet your sweet ass they have. And the very fact that she's still here and alive tells you that she must have passed."

He did wonder about that off and on for the next few hours. If they might have had someone do the check on her before he met her. It wouldn't have surprised him that someone in the family might have seen her coming to him and did all the background work beforehand. His family was scary smart about keeping secrets they didn't want anyone to mess with. Even though he was an immortal and the nephew of the king of all dragons, he was just a little kid when it came to the strength and power of his elders. Especially Uncle Cooper.

When his parents left, he and Shawn looked over the notes that he'd taken on his day in town. To him, it looked great, but Shawn wasn't having it. He wanted him to look at it like he was his equal. Not as some kid that came along when he fell in love with his mom.

"You don't believe that, do you? That you're here because of your mom and only that?" He shrugged and didn't look at him. "Shawn, I consider you my son. As much as if I'd fathered you. You are my boy. Even my family thinks of you as nothing but another Manning."

"The other kids, they told me that they're not treated any differently. I think that a few of them wanted to find out that you did. But I was told that they expect you to follow the rules just like everyone else and that you are just like everyone else, just like you said." Shawn finally looked up at him. "I'm not like the other kids, though, am I? I have magic. A grandfather that is a king of the fae. I was conceived by him because he was a mean and cruel man."

"To come to me." Shawn asked him what he meant. "Without all that happening—your mom being taken, you being conceived, it all had to work in a timeline that would bring you to this point you are at right now. My son. Son of your mother's too. A grannie that loves you so much that she'd easily die for you."

"She's related to me, so she has to feel that way." Dover leaned back on the couch, thinking about how to go about convincing Shawn that he was truly wanted. "It's all right, Dover. I'm all right with you and mom having other children too. I know that I'll never be your son. That's just the way it works with my friends."

"But you are my son." Dover didn't want to get upset with Shawn, but he didn't know how to make him understand that he would forever be his child. No matter the blood. "Did you know that Milo and George are adopted? That before they came to us, they were just humans?"

"I think that your mom told me that. She's a hoot." Dover agreed with him. Then asked if she or his dad treated them any differently. Shawn thought about it. "No. I guess they don't. Why not?"

"Because I love them as much as I do all the other children that I have." Mom kissed him on the cheek and then hugged Shawn. He had called for her help when he realized that he might be in over his head just enough to confuse Shawn. She was his hero, after all. "Shawn, none of my children are biologically mine. They're all random eggs that needed to be hatched and made a part of this world."

Shawn turned to look at him and then back at his mom. "Really? I mean, none of them?" She explained to him how she was only human, too, when she became a part of this family. "But you're not now, are you?"

"No. I'm the death watcher." While she explained to Shawn what that meant, Dover got up to find Toby. She'd been in the yard for some time now, and he wanted to make sure that she was all right. When he found her, he couldn't help but be happy that she was lying in the yard Letting the sun beat down on her face.

Toby looked incredibly relaxed right now. He opened the sliding door and sat down on one of the many chairs that had been recently put together. When she turned and looked at him, the smile she gave him was brighter than the sun.

"We should have sex soon." He asked her if right now was soon enough. "I think we should at least wait until Shawn and your mom is out—is it weird that I can feel her when she's nearby? I can actually feel all the dragons when they're close. Is that strange?"

"No. Not at all. It means that you're comfortable with them being there. I would say by the relaxed look on your face, that's how you feel anyway." He leaned back in the chair. "Will you marry me in a lavish wedding, or do you just want to file things at the courthouse that says that we're married and do the deed later?"

"Wow, I do hope your mother did a better job of teaching you to be romantic than that." She turned back to the sun. "I don't think that I'd like a big wedding. I doubt that anyone would come on my side but Grannie and Shawn. Your side would be full just by the sheer size of all of you. Then there—Dover, I'd like to have a child with you. Your mom explained to me that it would only be a one thing. George had set it up for all of you, but I'd like to have another child sooner rather than later. I don't want too many years between Shawn and a brother or sister."

"It's your body, honey. You tell me when and I'll be there with you all the way." She smiled but didn't look at him. "What are you thinking about? Something that I can help you with?"

"My father died last night. It should have happened a long time ago, but he had a massive stroke while fighting someone over their jello." She looked at him then. "I've not told anyone that I got the call. I went to see Grannie before coming out here, and she was in such a wonderful mood that I didn't say anything. She is in love with the apartment that you found for her. I think her being around other people her own age might — well, I was going to say mellow her, but I don't think that will happen, do you. She just says what she thinks."

"She does at that." She still looked sad, so he didn't think it was just her father passing. He'd been in prison for a very long time, and he doubted that she thought that much about him anymore. "Did you hear about what happened with your uncle? They say that he'll recover but that he's going to be in a great deal of pain for a long time. The catheter wasn't deflated before it was removed, and that caused him some serious damage to him."

"The hospital called yesterday to let us know. Grannie was going to go and see him today. She wants to be there when he finds out that his dick is no more useful than he ever was." They both laughed. "She also wants to get with one of your brothers that might have a law degree. She has to change out her will, and while she doesn't have a great deal of money, she doesn't want any of it to go to her sons. I told her that she should leave it for Shawn. He'd love that."

"Anyone of us has a law degree. Even my dad. He'd gladly do it for her. I think he finds her to be entertaining." Toby said that she could be mean when she wanted to be. "Yes. But never to family. I assume that you're talking about the other day at the school bus stop. I believe she was right in that the bus driver was at fault. There is an investigation going on now. But your grannie, she saved the day."

The bus driver had been screaming at the kids still on the bus when he let two kids off. Instead of paying attention to whether or not they'd gotten to their homes, he assumed so and nearly killed them both by lunging forward in the bus. Four of the passengers on the bus had fallen with scrapes and cuts, but it was Grannie that had grabbed up both of the children to safety.

"Shawn wants to go get pizza for dinner. If you don't mind." He said that he loved pizza. "He could eat it every meal now that he knows what a hot one tastes like. It's odd, don't you think that you think nothing of having a cold pizza being delivered from someplace. Then eating it in the restaurant that makes you not want to have it delivered ever again."

He helped her up off the lawn. And while she was close to him, he got himself a long kiss. Tasting her for later tonight. When she looked up at him, he smiled. Dover didn't think he could be more in love with his mate than he was at this moment.

~*~

That night Toby was going to stay in the master bedroom. She'd been coming in here to take a shower daily because of the way that water sprayed over her. But tonight, after taking a long hot bath, she decided that she was never going to sleep anywhere else in this house but in this room.

"I see that you beat me here." Toby's breath caught when she heard Dover's voice behind her. Turning slowly to have a good look at the man, she felt her mouth both dry out and salivate at the same time. "You keep looking at me like that, and I'm going to come all over you instead of inside of you like I've been thinking about for weeks."

"You're insane." He took a step toward her, gliding across the floor like he didn't need to touch his feet to the floor. "You're very handsome. I bet you hear that all the time."

"I don't. Not from anyone that counts. Other than my mom. But she doesn't tell me in the same tone that you just did. I want you." She said that she wanted him as well. "Good, at least we're on the same page. My mom wanted me to tell you that she and dad are going to keep Shawn all weekend. So if we had any plans with him, to cancel them. I think mom is very devious. How about you?"

"Devious? No. Smart, yes. I don't want to traumatize Shawn about his parents having sex until he's older." She was nearly to him when he stopped moving. "I want to touch all of you, but I'm having trouble thinking where to start."

"I'm going to start by asking you to make yourself naked." She was, and her thighs felt the cool air from the room. She was wet. And when Dover took in a deep breath, she knew that he was aware of how wet she was. "You smell like ambrosia. I'm going to eat as much of you as I can."

"Good." He picked her up then, laying her across the bed. She wasn't sure what to do with herself, but when he looked at her, Toby didn't think that she could do anything wrong. Just the way he was looking at her was enough to make her come. She let it go with a long, drawn-out moan.

"That's my girl. Don't hold back." He settled himself between her thighs and looked up at her. Running his hands up and down her legs, she could feel his hands getting closer and closer to her pussy. "Come again for me, love."

He devoured her then. Like she'd been on his plate, and he only just discovered that he was starving. Toby came so many times that she was overwhelmed with it. But she didn't ask him to stop. It was heaven, and he was hers.

While he fucked her with his fingers and tongue, she tried to capture a moment or two to catch her breath. Each time she came, screaming out his name, she begged him to stop. To give her a moment. But he was like a man on a mission to not miss anything about her while he was at his task. Finally, she couldn't wait any longer and pulled him up from her body by yanking his hair.

His face was covered in her cream. His lips were

swollen with his administrations, and she couldn't think of a more sexy thing. When he pulled her to him, kissing her with her cream still on his lips, Dover pulled her forward, off the bed to the floor. His cock, hard as any she'd ever seen, was right at her apex.

Lifting her up, she felt herself be impaled onto him. Screaming around the pleasure-pain of it, she held onto his shoulders as he bounced her up and down over him. Each time he took her breast into his mouth, she cried out. It wasn't that she enjoyed pain with her sex, but he was making her come by simply doing what he did best, be a beast to her body.

Once, she came so many times that she lost count, he laid her out on the floor. The pounding, there was no other word for it, was harder, more swift. Every time he touched her with his hands, running them up and down her body, she felt his body take her up another notch. As if he was getting her high enough to drop over the edge of something huge.

When he lifted her ass up to meet his downward strokes, it was all she could do to hang on. Making love like this was wonderfully fulfilling, and she couldn't wait for the next—

The room seemed to stretch out. Sound had no meaning. As Toby dug her nails into his back, holding onto him for whatever was coming next, she watched as the dust bunnies dancing around the room seemed to be reversing. Flying so slowly that there wasn't a time to measure it. Then the room, like a rubber band on a wrist, snapped back, and she was coming.

It seemed such a tamed word for how she was feeling. Every particle of her being was being slammed back together. Her hair even seemed to be screaming out its part in the climax. She would swear forever if asked that the floorboards beneath her seemed to be bracing itself for something more.

"Oh good Christ, Toby, I'm coming." It was as if she was accepting him when he did come. She held onto his body like a lifeline while he filled her. As he took her, over and over, emptying himself deep inside of her, she could feel creation. A child. Even as she was laid back gently on the floor, as if she were a treasured piece of jewelry, Toby watched Dover's face. He knew, too, was all she could think about.

When he put his hand over her belly, rising up just enough to look down at her, the tenderness after the way he'd taken her brought tears to her eyes. His kisses there had him rolling to his side and cuddling her to him so that he could touch her belly.

"A child is there. Our child." Toby put her hands over his and held him there. "I didn't know what to expect, to be honest with you. I mean, I had no idea that it would be...I feel like I've been given a great gift in knowing that I'm going to be having the first child born of a hatchling and a human."

"Do you think that she'll be some fae?" It *was* a girl too. While she didn't know how she knew that, it was indeed a female child. Dover nodded. "She'll be a princess. Our fae princess with our prince son."

"She'll be beautiful like her mom. Strong like you too." The two of them lay there for an hour, talking about what their daughter would have. The things that Shawn would teach her. As the floor seemed to get harder beneath her, she decided to get up and get into the nice soft bed.

"I'm not sure how this works with having a child." She cocked a brow at him. "I mean, I know how babies are born, but I know nothing about how our child will be born. I'm assuming, for some reason, that it will be born as a human will be. But I haven't any idea. I do know that when a dragon has an egg, it's small. Then as the dragon grows, so does the egg. That's about the extent of my knowledge of dragon babies."

"That's more than I knew. I wonder if it will take nine months or — how long is a dragon pregnant for?" He shrugged. "I can see you're going to be a great deal of help as we go along, aren't you?"

"Mom has a book, but I don't think there will be much in there that we can use with our baby. As I said, you're the first." He kissed her belly again and then stood up. "I'm starving."

They made their way to the kitchen, stopping every few steps to touch one another. Once they were in the kitchen, food all over the counter, trying to decide what they wanted, the two of them decided that they wanted to get into the pool. That was a huge mistake, as it turned out.

The water was spilled all over the yard. More than half the water was splashed out when Dover decided that he wanted to cool off his dragon feet. When he told her about Finn's need for cold water, she laughed so hard at thinking about Finn melting a piece of iron to make a point to some idiots.

"He hates to do that. All of us hate to use force like that. But sometimes you have to get their attention before you can get anything done." She agreed with him. It was like that as a teacher. "I don't know how you do it as a teacher, love. I don't. I've been one before in my lifetime and vowed never again. They're the — to me, the most disrespected people ever born."

"I don't know about all that, but I do know that when you find that one student, you feel like it's all worth it." Talking about this and that, she realized that she'd eaten as much as Dover had. She'd been hungry, of course, but that didn't explain how the two of them had been able to finish off ten pounds of lunch meat in a single setting.

They made love several more times. Nothing like the first time but just as fulfilling. Twice he devoured her, and she was able to have him come down her throat too. She thought that it was the most fun she'd ever had during sex. And felt second nature to her. Like they'd been making love every night forever. She told Dover what she'd been thinking.

"George told me once that he thought that making

love with your mate was akin to becoming alive for the first time. I hadn't any idea what he meant, thinking he was off his noodle or something being in love." She asked him what he thought now. "That it had it perfectly right when he described it that way. It's not like you were dead to feelings before, but you're more alive with the ones that you have now. Understand?"

"I do." They finished off a cake that had been in the freezer. While she hadn't any idea why there was a cake there, they demolished it in no time. Frozen be damned. "I'm stuffed. Let's go back to bed and start over again tomorrow. I want to pretend that the world doesn't exist beyond our door."

"Deal." Dover looked at her with a wink before picking her up in his arms to carry her up the stairs. "We do have things that have to be taken care of in the afternoon. But I think I'll have you well satisfied before then. Especially if we work really hard on keeping our bodies ready all the time."

Life was much too enjoyable to sleep it away, she discovered. And while she settled down to nap, suddenly very tired, she thought of all the things that she wanted to do now that she'd have her family around her. The first and foremost thing she wanted to do was keep memories alive by taking pictures.

People had them on their phones. She knew that. But she wanted some that she could hold in her hands. Hang on the wall too. Thinking of how she had a frame that would hold several paintings that Shawn did for her in school, she wondered if they had something like that for photos too. It was worth looking into.

As she drifted off to sleep, wrapped up in Dover's arms, Toby thought of her father one more time.

He would miss everything. But the more she thought about it, the more she realized that he'd already missed a great deal. He'd been in prison this time for the last twelve years and, at the time of his death, had two more life sentences to go. There was nothing that she could do about it either. Toby didn't care that he'd done this all on his own, either. Then there was her uncle and his life choices. It was his life. He was the one that was going to have to live with the consequences of his actions. Toby found that she just didn't care.

Tomorrow was a new day, and she was going to start living it on her own terms with Dover and their family at her side. Yes, she thought. Life was going to get pretty exciting soon, and she couldn't wait to be able to participate in it.

Chapter 7

Grannie watched her idiot son sleep. He'd been coming in and out of it since she'd shown up an hour ago. The dumb fuck. What did he expect to happen to him when he got himself in a mess in the first place. When she looked at him, he was staring at her like he didn't have a clue who she might be.

"I'm your momma, you moron." He asked her why she had to be so mean all the time. "You've driven me to it. You and that fucking brother of yours. Why I was saddled with the two of you and not at least one of you being a nice one is beyond me. But it don't matter now. Are you awake enough to listen to me now?"

"You said that to me before?" She nodded and asked him if he was ready again. "I suppose so. I'm not going to prison. I want you to make arrangements for me to get out of here. Me and Daniel, we're going to need some seed money too, so don't you be holding back on us."

"Daniel is dead." He asked her what she'd said to him. "Like I've told you every time you tell me not to hold out on you. Daniel. Is. Dead. He had himself a heart thing happen, and it killed him right then. You might want to heed what happened to him if you want to be around much—"

"You're a liar." Grannie stood up and went to her son, and punched him right in the face. She was glad to see that his head bounced back, so it looked like she'd been able to get in two punches rather than just the one. "What did you do that for?"

"I am not a liar, you fuck tard. I've told you this several times now, and you'll listen better now. He's dead. And you are, too, going to prison. For a long time. Also, you might want to take some stock in that dick of yours." He asked her what was wrong with it. "You know what you did. You pulled that plunger thing right out through your pecker until it was nearly nothing but raw meat. Go ahead and have yourself a look-see."

"I don't wanna." She told him to suit himself. That she'd taken pictures of it. "Why would you do that? What are you going to do with pictures of my dick?"

"Show kids what happens to you when you don't do what you're told. I don't know. I think I could make a mint off of telling kids what not to do like you boys did." She hadn't taken a picture. Not even taken a peek at his wiener. She just wanted to upset him. "I'm here to tell you too that once you're in prison, don't be expecting me to come around. I'm an old woman, and I've washed my hands of the two of you anyway. You're nearly old enough to get one of those checks each month, and you still haven't figured out how to hold down a job. Dumbass. Donald, what the hell would you be doing right now if you weren't a lifer? You ain't going to be bumming around with me."

"You're my momma. You're going to take care of me until I say differently." Grannie rolled her eyes hard enough for them to have heard it down the hall. "Why are you really in here? Treating me like this? Did Toby kick you to the side of the road yet? I would have."

"She's married herself up a few notches above being rich. Married her a man that has more money than even all the banks in the world would be having. And I love him like my own son. Not like you, morons. Shawn is happy too, in case you were wondering." He told her that he wasn't. "I didn't think you would be. But she's got herself a nice man, a lot of money, and she don't mind sharing it with her grannie either. The bloodline must have skipped over her when she was being created. I used to think that she wasn't going to amount to much, not with her daddy like he was, but I'm right happy with her. And that boy of hers, he's a keeper too."

"Like I care. She'd better be forking out some money when I get out of here. I'm not saying that you're not telling me the truth about Daniel, but I want her to make sure that I live in the lap of food too." She corrected him. "I don't want no luxury, damn it. I want food and a place to sleep at night that don't have rats as big as my head wanting a part of me."

"You're a fool. I've always known that. Even your daddy knew it. But you're a bigger fool if you think that she's going to be coming around to help you out. She's happy. And while I'd like to warn you to stay away from her, I also know that there ain't no way that you're going to be getting to her anyway." Grannie, all she'd been called since she'd had her first son, stood up. "You have yourself whatever life you deserve, Donald. Not that I care a fig newton if you do or not. But you think on how much fun we're having every time you have those bars slam shut on your ass every day."

She was still giggling as she walked out of the hospital. There were six guards entering the room that she had left to keep an eye on Donald until he was moved. It couldn't be soon enough for her, she thought.

There was a big limo there waiting for her when she came out of the hospital. Getting inside of it, she was thrilled to pieces that Shawn was there waiting for her. He was telling her about all the things that he was going to do with her tonight that they'd planned. The kid, he was so much like his mother that she didn't care how he was conceived.

"Oh, the man that was trying to take the teapot from Mr. Cooper has been found. The big dummy wanted it so that no one else could have it. He was going to break it up so he'd be the last person to touch it. Isn't that stupid?" Grannie agreed but thought maybe it was a bit more than that. But she didn't say anything to Shawn. "When school starts up, I'm going to be going to a private school so that I'll be safe. There won't be anyone to come and get me but you and mom and Dover."

"You going to call him Dover or dad? Seems to me that he's been better to you than any father that you could have had." Shawn told her he was still thinking on it. "Well, don't wait too long. You surely will make that man's day if you were to call him that. I know you already feel it."

"I do. I'm glad that he makes mom happy too. Do you think they'll have a baby?" She'd bet her last nickel that if she wasn't knocked up by now, Toby surely would be soon. "I would love a little brother. I don't know about a sister. Levi has one of them, and all she wants him to do with her is play tea with her. I play with her sometimes when I go over there. She sure is bossy about fake tea, I think."

He told her about the things that his friend Levi had at his house. Which didn't seem like all that much to her. She might have to have a look-see or have Toby do it to see if they didn't have enough food around. Shawn had told her twice now that the kid was forever starving when he came to their house for the afternoon.

By the time she was ready to call it a day, she and Shawn had gotten her bedroom unpacked and the bed put together. She was going to make sure that she put the rest of the furniture together when he went home. Settling down to have some popcorn and watch a movie, Grannie was happy with her own four walls.

It had never bothered her to share her home with Toby and her little boy. She loved the two of them like they were her own children. She supposed in some way they were. But now that she'd been given herself her own place and pretty things in it, she was glad now that Shawn was willing to stay here rather than her having to go to the big house. Not that she didn't love it there, but this was her home. A place where she could just be Grannie Deaver.

~*~

Colby put the last of the root veggies in the cellar and locked the door. She had a lot of things to get taken care of over the next few days, and leaving the pumpkins and yams to lie in the sun wasn't going to make her happy when she returned. Picking up her bag, she made her way to her bike. She thought it had attributed it to her long life, riding the sucker around for miles and miles a day.

Harry was just where he said he'd be, at the end of the five-mile driveway waiting on her. He was a good boy, her nephew. A little on the oddish side, but he was the only other living relative that she had. And he wanted nothing to do with her plans for her family land.

"I could have come up the driveway after you, Aunt Colby. The car will take the drive." She said that if she'd not ridden her bike down the drive, she'd have nothing to drive back up. "Yes, well, I can take you up the drive, too, when you return. Do you have your money?"

"I do. You said that I'd be able to catch a flight out today. Is that still true?" He told her that the plane going to Ohio was departing at five tonight. "Then I'll be on it. I should have done this weeks ago, but I kept putting it off."

"I do that too. When I have a task that I don't want

to do, I put it off until it's almost too late. I did want to run something by you on the way to the airport. You said you were going to see the Mannings, correct?" She said that it was the name on the paperwork that her great-grandmother had saved. "Yes, well, before you go all the way there and back, I think they might well be around here. About an hour's drive. That's why I wanted to come and get you early."

She'd not been in town for a while now. Not since her grandmother had passed away two summers ago. Looking out the window, knowing that it would hurt Harry if he saw her crying, she thought about how much she missed every one of her family and now, well, at ninety-six, she had to think practically with her head and not with her heart.

"Look over there." The sign was as big as she was, and she thought it looked like the same logo that had been on the paperwork she had on her. "We'll just ask around. If they're only just now setting up an office, perhaps they can let you talk to them, and there wouldn't be any reason for you to fly out there."

He didn't want her to leave. Colby knew this. Every day he'd call her, asking after her to make sure that she was still alive. The two-way street of it only being the two of them left hurt them both a great deal.

Getting out of the car, she was always slightly nauseous when she could smell the smells of the town. Being on the farm without the unwanted benefit of having smog all around her, she thought that, too, had a great deal to do with her being still alive. But then, all her family members on the Wiffle side lived to be over a hundred. She caught up with Harry when he was speaking to a nice-looking couple.

"I'm afraid that Uncle Cooper isn't here today, but he can be here tomorrow if you'd like to wait on him to talk to him. It would certainly save you a trip all the way to his home. If you don't mind, can I ask you what this might be about?" Harry turned to her when the man asked her. "I don't have to know. I can just tell him you need to see him. My name is Dover, by the way, Dover Manning."

"The dragons." He didn't bother looking around. She'd said it so low that she doubted that Harry could have heard her. But the man had. She knew it. "Mr. Manning and my great so far back grandmother it's been so long were friends of a sort. Well, back a long way from just her. My family knew your uncle when he was merely starting out in the world. Her name would have been Alma Wiffle."

"He talks about her." She nodded, knowing that at some point, her family would have been brought up. Let me get in touch with him, and I'll see what he wants to do. Are you staying here in town?"

"No. We're just a few miles out of town. Still on the same land that we've always been on." He nodded, as if he knew just what she was talking about. "If you'd let him know that I can meet him anytime, I'd surely appreciate it." He asked for a moment, and after telling him to go on, she looked at the building that they were all standing in front of.

The young woman, Toby, was talking to Harry about it. Colby walked away just to have herself a sit down while she waited on the younger man.

She was sure that he was a dragon as well. While she had no way of telling the difference between humans and other creatures, she knew that the Manning dragons were a strong race of beings. Colby had hoped that, at some point, she could show him the pictures and drawings of him and his brothers that had been made so long ago. When a shadow fell over her, Colby lifted her face to see who it might be.

"Hello, Colby." She nodded to the handsome stranger knowing that she was in the presence of someone great. "You look a great deal like your grandmother. She forever had white hair too. She told me once that it was because she'd been worrying over us for so long. But I think she was born with it."

"She was. All of the firstborn females of the Whiffle family were. I'm the last one of them." He told her that he was sorry. "No need for that. Now, you and my grannie had an agreement, so to speak. I'm here to let you take over the farm."

"I don't remember all the details, but I do remember it being deemed that once your family line was finished, which I don't see as a possibility with your nephew still a young man, then the land and all that was there would be the Mannings. Do you remember why we did it that way? I'm foggy on the details without my notes in front of me." She told him that Harry wanted nothing to do with producing children. Nor did he want to be around the family land at all. "I see. He's aware of the terms of the pact that we have."

"He is. We've all been aware of it. If you don't want it, the city will take it, and it will sit useless for the rest of your life. I've no doubt that will be long after I'm dust." She tried for humor, but it fell flat. "I'm behind on the taxes as of this quarter. I tried to make it, but nobody wants fresh anymore when they can have it packaged up and brought to their door for nothing. Waste of time and money, if you ask me when it's all right there for the growing, but I'm from a different timeline than these people are."

"As am I." Cooper was a handsome man. As handsome as the pictures that she had of him. After talking them out of the satchel she'd brought and handing them over to him, she sat there while he looked them over. "These are wonderful. I can see my brothers here. The artist did a good job of it."

"There are no dragon pictures, of course. You were just starting out, and she wanted to capture you all in the right time of your life. I'm told that she treasured these above that of her own children's drawings." He smiled at one of the pictures, but she didn't ask him. "I'm an old woman, Mr. Manning and have lived a great and wonderful life. But my time to marry and have children is well past that time. I'm here to turn over what I have to you so that someday, someone might remember how to put the plow to earth and sow a nice garden."

"We'll do just that with the land." She knew that too. They'd not be splitting it up, either. Nor would there be any malls or apartments on the land. It was going to be a lasting testimony of how the earth looked thousands of years ago. A working farm for people to see, experience and to use. She could see it in her mind.

The barns that had fallen into disrepair would be made whole again. The orchards where the grapes, apples and other trees grew would be plentiful. There'd be no faeries either, working the land. It was for humans, for them to learn a valuable lesson. A lesson of making sure that you support and feed yourself if necessary.

They talked over some of the finer points until Cooper asked her again why they had made the deal. Colby had a feeling that he knew just why, but he wanted to hear her version of it. One that had been passed down from generation to generation.

"You and your brothers came upon a small child.

She was nothing more than a weed herself, she told me when she saw these great dragons carrying themselves across the land exhausted." Closing her eyes, she remembered in detail as if she'd been there with them. "With the help of her parents, they nursed you along, keeping you safe and out of harm's way until you could make your way across the states to Ohio. In payment, you told her that you would supply her with riches to keep the land productive. While she told you there was no reason for you to do it, my relative made sure that not only were you provided with the things that you needed, but they also made sure that you had things you'd need to blend in with others. They made you your first shirts and pants. Fitted you for shoes and hats. My family, blessed as they were, helped you, and you felt the need to return the favor. But instead, they decided that should their line ever exhaust out, you'd come and take over, to give the land what it needed to survive as she had helped you six do in those years."

"She taught us how to garden. What was needed in the way of speech. Your grannie told us about lambs and cattle and how just eating them wasn't enough. They had to be replenished, or we'd starve. Same with the gardens. The trees and lakes." She nodded. Then pulled out the last thing that she'd brought for him. "My scale."

"Yes. Is yours now. We had generations of children born into the family because of this. Leaving it for us, only needing to touch the beautiful colors to be able to conceive, had kept the line going for this long." He asked about her. "I had no husband that lived long enough to be with me. He died the day we were wed when a man robbed us. My heart, it was broken, never to be filled again. I am the last Alma Colby Margaret Wiffle to be born."

She stayed in a hotel room that night. After meeting all the dragons and telling the same stories over and over, Colby was exhausted. At ninety-seven, she was far too old for much in the way of frivolity. Closing her eyes that night, a smile on her lips, she dreamed a dream like she'd never dreamed before of a life with children at her feet and dragons at her beck and call.

There were beautiful children everywhere. Some of them older, and others are just infants. Several with the brightest white hair that she'd ever seen. The flowers around the homestead were beautiful. Gardens of tomatoes and green beans were in neat rows. She even loved how the wisteria grew along the porch roof without intruding on the floorboards. It was perfect. As she had never dreamed of it before.

On some level, Colby knew that she had died. Knew it in her heart that this dream, or whatever it was, it was showing her that she'd made the right decision. Of course, that didn't explain why the children were everywhere. Nor why the homestead looked so lovely and full. But she didn't care. If heaven was going to be like this, she could surely be here forever.

There were dragons on the land. Small ones that were giving rides to the small ones. Goats, too, that had faeries riding them. The air smelled so fresh that she found herself wishing that she could take in one more breath before it all disappeared.

There were steaks on the grill. A pig being roasted over a spit. Food, so many covered dishes that she thought that there would be leftovers for months. Bowls of fresh fruit, apples the size of her fist. Peaches were so juicy that she was sure that it was going to be more mess than eating them. Still, she didn't care.

Seeing Cooper and the other Mannings sitting under

a tree, she made her way there. Being dead didn't offer her any kind of magical knowledge she didn't think. But she knew these men to be his brothers as much as she knew Harry to be her nephew. It was just the way that it should have been.

"You'll depart soon?" She told Cooper that she didn't want to think on leaving here anytime soon. "You'll return."

"Nay, I will not. But the memories that I have will last me several lifetimes, don't you think?" He laughed. A little nervously, but he laughed all the same. "I shall miss this place more than ever now. It is a place that I shall think of often if there is an afterlife. Thank you for this."

"I did nothing, Colby. You have done this all on your own. Well, not entirely. The magic that you returned to me, it had a great deal to do with it." She didn't understand but didn't care. She was here, and that was all that mattered to her. "Have a wonderful trip."

She would too. But later. As she made her way back to the house, taking in as much as she could, Colby decided that if she were able to paint or draw like her relatives had been able to do all those years ago, this was just what she'd paint. The house, the trees and the family that she had — in just a few seconds — fallen in love with.

Before You Go...

HELP AN AUTHOR

write a review

THANK YOU!

Share your voice and help guide other readers to these wonderful books. Even if it's only a line or two, your reviews help readers discover the author's books so they can continue creating stories that you'll love. Log in to your favorite retailer and leave a review. Thank you.

AWARD WINNING, BESTSELLING AUTHOR

Kathi Barton, a winner of the Pinnacle Book Achievement Award and a best-selling author on Amazon and All Romance books, lives in Nashport, Ohio, with her husband, Paul. When not creating new worlds and romance, Kathi and her husband enjoy camping and going to auctions. She can also be seen at county fairs with her husband, who is an artist and potter.

Her muse, a cross between Jimmy Stewart and Hugh Jackman, brings her stories to life for her readers in a way that has them coming back time and again for more. Her favorite genre is paranormal romance, with a great deal of spice. You can visit Kathi online and drop her an email if you'd like. She loves hearing from her fans. aaronskiss@gmail.com.

Follow Kathi on her blog: http://kathisbartonauthor.blogspot.com/